THE ARCHITECT

BOOK 1: THE ORIGIN

KEN TATE
DUKE TATE

The Architect
Book 1: The Origin

Copyright © 2021 by Ken Tate and Duke Tate

ISBN 978-1-951465-49-0 ebook
ISBN 978-1-951465-50-6 paperback
ISBN 978-1-951465-51-3 hardcover

Pearl Press, LLC
PO Box 2036
Del Ray Beach, Florida
33483

Dedicated to my mother, Gene

*"What if you slept and what if
In your sleep you dreamed
And what if in your dream
You went to heaven
And there plucked
A strange and beautiful flower
And what if when you awoke
You had that flower in your hand
Ah, what then?"*

—Samuel Taylor Coleridge

---

*"I did not write half of what I saw, for I knew I would not be
believed."*

—Marco Polo

CONTENTS

1

October 1st, 1901

On a misty morning hike up the highest point of the mountain, above the lush acreage he had recently purchased along the Napali coast of Kauai, Hawaii, Fernando Serrano—a towering Spaniard who could beat anyone at a navaja knife throw—heard the most majestic sounds emanating from up the narrow dirt path ahead of him. Unlike anything he had ever heard before, the mesmerizing sound drew him to it. He stopped for a moment to listen, trying to detect what direction it was coming from. Dropping his canvas satchel, he followed it, trailing off the path up the rugged mountain—the sound becoming more audible as he approached it.

In a moment, he reached a small, narrow cave. Right as he ducked inside, a feral pig squealed as it darted out of the opening. He jumped back out alarmed. Regaining his composure, he looked in the hole again. It was pitch black, but the ethereal sound continued from inside. He entered the mouth of the cave, and the beautiful music was at full volume as he made his way towards it. In the distance, he noticed the source of the sound also seemed to be radiating a warm glow that got brighter as he neared.

When he reached the object, he observed that it was some kind of a majestic black stone he had never ever seen before. The light and sound radiated from the interior core upwards, filling the space around it with an aural blue and white light. He kneeled down beside it in awe and when his shaking fingers touched it, the world went black.

October Ist, 2021

Meg Summers slammed the snooze button, sighed a grizzly groan and squeezed the leopard-skin patterned pillow to her ears on both sides, "Another brutal day in the East Coast world of buildings!"

Why couldn't she just be a coffee barista in Montauk? Give surf lessons in her spare time and live in a cute little above-garage apartment. She was thirty-seven, with her whole life ahead of her.

Leaning up, she stared lucidly at one of her fantasy drawings, executed with magic markers and pens on butcher paper framed in a heroic gold leaf. This particular drawing from her time at Yale Architectural School was her favorite of the series because it was of a whimsical palace set in a tropical forest. When she saw it in her dreams, the palace always had a mystical theater with a dome that showed the twinkling sky at night; she often saw herself as a star dancing the polished stage floor with a man, but she could never see his face. She would be barefoot and free without all the silly rules she had grown up with—attending Cotillion classes in Newport, Rhode Island with her overbearing mother, Scarlett, who had forced her into this grueling profession.

The nerve she had, Meg thought. Why me? She had even pressured her to go to Yale. She had really wanted to attend the Rhode Island School of Design where all her artsy friends had gone, but her Mom said that she would rather die than watch her daughter attend a school where everyone did dope.

Meg's rocky marriage to one of the richest guys at Yale, Mick Drewford, had skidded to an abrupt halt last year when she caught him in the back seat of his vintage fire-engine red Mercedes with her younger sister, Dawn. At that moment, her whole life drifted away like a boat sent out to sea, leaving her hopelessly alone on a barren shore.

The last seven years of her life had been devoted to creating sublime houses and estates across America, but now it was a distraction from the pain of her sister and husband's affair. On the inside, she felt empty because she was alone, and managing people at her office and on construction sites tore her soul apart.

Yes, Meg Summers really was born to draw—she loved to draw buildings, dreaming of shapes and colors, in a landscape of unfettered creativity. In her current profession as an architect, she only ever got to spend a small amount of time drawing the house during the design phase—the rest of the time felt wasted, managing her staff, the builders and landscape architect. She had once hired a manager named Craig to oversee the construction of her projects, but he simply couldn't answer the tough questions about details the builders had, so she eventually had to let him go.

While driving around town, she constantly edited and fixed existing buildings in her mind, correcting the windows and porticos. She thought of nothing but buildings.

She hopped out of bed and attacked the morning like she

did every day since graduating pre-school. She had never missed a day of work. Propelling her lanky but defined thirty-seven-year-old figure—cute to most men, but horrid to her—across the floor to her luxuriously appointed white marbled bathroom, she completed her morning ritual with exact execution. Meg was tall, had dark brown hair, hazel eyes and an angular face and body.

First up was the shower. For any architect, a shower must be a crucial part of the day, Meg thought. Her whole life was about houses and their structure. The bathroom was a sacred place for washing and cleaning the soul's vehicle. Grooming was exceptionally important too, so closets were high on the list. Hers, a walk-in with mahogany doors and an exquisite island in the center with lovely shelves to store all her vintage sunglasses and cute eyewear, was her favorite part of the home. Kitchens and dining rooms are the heart of a dwelling because that's where families came together to celebrate, wine and dine, and share stories. Hers was empty most of the time, so she avoided it like the plague. Living rooms were for relaxing and unwinding, and studies and libraries were for learning and expanding one's knowledge. For Meg, every room of a house was linked to a specific aspect of a person that corresponded to its function. The windows were the eyes, the door the mouth, the attic where all the distant memories were held, and the basement, well, no one goes there, Meg thought.

She showered and went into the grand closet where she chose a starched white button-up from a row of fifty identical ones, stiff khaki pants from a similar row and a pair of round tortoise-rimmed Vint and York glasses from her island drawer. Five sprays of Chanel No. 5 and she was already moving on to the kitchen where she prepared a plate of her standard two boiled free-range eggs, which she peeled and salted with French sea salt.

Meg had the same thing every day for breakfast, never veering. Simplicity was the essence of life, she always said.

The drive to work in her 2020 ice-white Mercedes SUV along the East Hampton coast on this crisp autumn day was short with no traffic, as she preferred it to be. Her office was downtown in a nice, manicured white clapboard cottage with a matching picket fence and red rose bushes perfuming the front porch. The rooms of the bungalow housed her head renderer and designer, Sam and Mal, while her production architects Bob, Taylor, Susan and Alexandria worked remotely from their Manhattan lofts.

Walking in, her secretary, Peggy, greeted her with her standard exuberant charm. Peg was a thirty-one-year-old curly-haired blonde, blue-eyed, cherub-faced valley girl from Los Angeles whose spritely attitude had a special way of putting a smile on Meg's face.

"Good morning Meg."

"Good morning Peg!"

"How was your weekend?"

"Oh okay, same old same old, you know. Any calls?"

"Yeah, one from a Mr. Billsworth. Said he wanted to speak to you about renovating some brownstone on the Upper West Side."

"Great, email me his info."

"Okay Meg, will do."

"Thanks."

3

In Meg's office—decorated with many hand-drawn framed renderings of their projects by Sam, along with antique drawings of Italian villas she purchased on her most recent trip to Florence, Italy, which she took alone—she slipped into her sleek vintage office chair and pulled up her iMac. She shuffled through her inbox. A few emails were praise from colleagues for winning the prestigious Academy of Architecture Award the previous month for a shingle-style house on the shore of Nantucket, then a few painstaking emails from Bob and Taylor in Manhattan—so boring, Meg thought. She opened the Mr. Billsworth email. Then, she worked throughout the morning on a hectic project in Manhattan with Mal until lunch.

Her head designer Mallory Jackson—or Mal for short—was driving her crazy today on the detailing for the house, which was a complete gut and redo. They were redesigning the entire interior down to the studs. It was still a Federal design, but more high style with many more expensive details, materials and hardware.

Like Meg, Mallory had graduated from Yale. She wore black

every day of the week. She had spiked hair and argued with everything Meg asked her to do. Mallory was a "no" person, meaning that "no" was the first response out of her mouth every time someone asked her a question. But she was a genius at design, and even though she had searched the world over, Meg could never find anyone to replace her.

Today, Meg's neck was sore from the back-and-forth emails with Mal about mistake after mistake. She poured another iced latte in the office kitchen brewed from Arabica beans—a habit she had developed early on in her career to keep her analytical left-brain thinking sharp. Then she exited the office for lunch. Peg had already left to go eat or Meg would have asked her to come along. She liked Peg, not just because their names rhymed, but she was chipper and upbeat, the polar opposite of Mal.

Gray clouds were building in the distant sky as she walked down the picturesque Hamptons sidewalk to her favorite lunch place, the Saltbox Café, where she ate every day, rain or shine. Routine was the essence of simplicity, and simplicity was the essence of life.

The Hamptons café was packed on this first day of October. A lanky surfer with a backwards Quicksilver ball cap and navy hoodie stood at the back of the line with his girlfriend, who sported a dirty-blonde ponytail and white cable crew sweater. Meg filed in behind them.

While waiting, she opened her Moleskine notebook and glanced at her most recent fantasy sketch. When it was her time to order, she was not hungry for the Saltbox anymore, but something more Hawaiian, like lomi lomi salmon. Those brats in front of her had made her wish she was sitting on the beach with a Mai Tai instead of stuck in New York on a gray day.

As fate would have it, she stepped up and ordered her usual —a tuna sandwich with melted Swiss cheese on gourmet rye with a dill pickle and a side of organic coleslaw—and took her seat at the same spot in the cozy corner she sat in every day (as long as it wasn't taken by someone else).

Black-and-white photographs hung on the walls: old salty seadogs and wooden boats on the horizon were neatly framed in a light wood painted matte white. They were accompanied by vintage oars and casting nets from a bygone era. The smell of fried cod and cottage-cut french fries wafted through the air.

Meg opened her Moleskine and started a new sketch. This one she thought would be the drawing of a lifetime. A building for the ages.

After drawing freehand for about twenty minutes, she had a masterpiece underway. Mitch, a surfer with shaggy brown hair and blue eyes who always waited on her, delivered her tuna sandwich. "Thanks Mitch," she said to him and he winked and replied, "No problem Meg."

While she ate, she fantasized about drawing the rest of the building. She was dreaming the house like she always did. This one was different than the others: grand, more palatial, with towers and domes like some of her college fantasy drawings, and it climbed a tropical mountain. It was like something out of the *Arabian Nights* and fit for a queen. After sketching for a little longer, she finished the initial draft, signed her name at the right-hand corner and left (*Figure 1*).

Figure 1 *Meg's Moleskine Sketch of a fantasy building with domes and towers*

4

At two pm, Mal buzzed Meg with a technical question about an arch detail on the Upper West Side project. Walking down the hall, Meg reluctantly turned into Mal's office.

Mal, whose face looked angelic like a fairy, could have been a model with her slender frame if she had been taller, but she obscured her beauty with her geeky hairdo, zero make up and a constant frown.

Today, she had on her usual big, black Skull Candy headphones and was dressed head to toe in black: skinny jeans, furry Ugg boots, and a long-sleeved designer cashmere sweater. Each was of a different shade of darkness. Meg sometimes thought Mal believed she was a beatnik or something, but her personality was more Goth than beat. Meg actually loved the beats: Kerouac, Ferlinghetti and Alan Watts were some of her favorite writers. She had read them all in high school, as well as Henry Miller books of essays like *The Wisdom of the Heart* when she wanted to get away from the mundane preppy East Coast life she was born into—a revolving door of Ivy-league football tailgates at Yale, foie gras toasties, polished silver and equestrian lessons. She could not stand the thought of that disgusting foie gras her father, James, loved so much. To think anyone would force-feed an animal to fatten its liver so it could be killed for the taste...so inhumane.

"Show me the detail please, Mal," Meg requested, standing over Mal's right shoulder.

Mal could not hear a word Meg was saying over the racket pumping into her head, probably the Dead Kennedys or Iron Maiden. Meg raised her voice and shouted, "What are you working on, Mal?"

Mal caught Meg's glance and removed her Skull Candy headphones, letting them rest on her neckline.

"Oh, hey Meg. Just the details for the foyer on the 55th Avenue project." Death metal banging out of the headphones on her neck at an ungodly decibel.

Meg studied the Auto Cad drawings carefully. Mal had totally botched the moldings and the stair railing as well.

"No, this can't be. If you have not done so already, you need to research Mott Schmidt's Federal Townhouse for Anne Morgan on Sutton Place and study his foyer details. They are lighter and more elegant than the ones you've drawn here. Just throw these away and start over!"

After arguing with Mal for some time, Meg left the room distraught. She walked around the corner to Sam Babson's office to regain some positivity after Mal's gloom.

Sam, the most stylish employee of the office, did all the firm's renderings. Unlike their competitors in Manhattan, he still did them in colored pencil, the old-fashioned way. They were truly fabulous.

An eccentric gay man from Dothan, Alabama, he was Southern as the day was long. Today, he was dressed in a baby-blue seersucker suit with a red paisley vintage bow tie. Perched on top of his drafting board on all fours with a pair of clear painting googles wrapped over his hazel eyes, the country group Brooks and Dunn's song *"Brand New Man"* was playing on a small Bluetooth retro speaker. Meg observed that Sam was staring directly into his drafting light.

"Sam?" At the sound of her voice, he turned his head to take her in. "What are you doing on top of the table like that?"

"Why, I am changing the lightbulb darling. You know, if you're not careful, these things can just explode on you." At that moment, as if by some command from the sound of his voice, the lightbulb exploded, covering Sam and the room in white powder.

"Oh, my goodness!" Meg exclaimed, recoiling around the corner from the mess and shielding her eyes. When the dust settled, she slowly eased back in the door.

"See? I told you so, sweetie."

"I guess so, Sam." She gave him a cute smile and walked away back to her office, shaking her head all the while in complete disbelief.

5

A thunderstorm brewed outside Meg's office window. She had the radio dialed to her favorite channel, Island Life. "Surf's Up" by the Beach Boys—one of her favorite songs—was playing. When it ended, Hugh Stewart, Montauk's own surf DJ, asked the audience, "How would you like to escape this brutal gray New York weather to visit the beautiful islands of Hawaii?" Yes please, thought Meg. Hugh then described a fully paid week's vacation to the garden isle of Kauai that he was going to give away to the first caller who could name Martin's dog from the popular 90s sitcom *Frasier*, which he said was set in drizzly Seattle.

"Eddie, it's Eddie!" said Meg. Not the type to call in to a radio show for a million reasons, she smiled and glanced at her modern Nelson Ball clock—one of 150 clocks designed by George Nelson for the Howard Miller Clock Company in 1949.

It read 4:12. Time for her to go.

She loved to depart early: first one to leave, first one home.

The storm was the perfect excuse to duck out. She turned off her desktop computer, flipped the switch on the light, put on her raincoat and raced down the hall past Mal, skipping joyfully past Sam's office as well. She didn't want to chat today. As she zoomed past Peg, she gave her a quick, "Ciao, girl." After she walked out the front door, Sam opened it, still wearing the protective googles, and called out to her in the street, "Darling, where are you going so early?"

"I can't talk Sam. Can't you see it's raining?"

"Okay girl, but wear your wellies next time!" He waved.

"You know me. Always prepared." She smiled, hopped into her Mercedes and sped off down the street.

She wanted to stop at The Nook and Cranny Rare Used Bookstore and find some gem on fabulous Middle Eastern palaces to get inspiration for her fantasy drawings. She could not find a single parking space on the side of the street where The Nook was located. Cursing her luck, she parked on the opposite side. She reached for her Scalamandre red zebra-printed umbrella in the backseat, but it was missing. Must have left it at the house, she thought. She grabbed the *New York Times* Arts & Leisure section and held it over her head as she ran across the street in between honking horns.

"Sorry guys, sorry."

When she walked in, a bell on the door chimed. Mr. Bartholmey, whom everyone called Bart, was the storeowner, and a mainstay in town. He wore a canvas work apron every day for no apparent reason, except that it let everyone know he worked there when he was stocking books. And perhaps he thought that the ensemble made him look old-timey.

Meg ordered an iced latte to go at the café in the back of the store and proceeded to cruise through the architecture sections. The bookstore was jam-packed with first editions. They even had a gold-leafed version of Sir Richard Burton's *A Thousand and One Nights* in all its seventeen-volume glory up front right next to a gleaming copy of James Joyce's *Ulysses*. She loved the smell of old books and the feel of the pages.

She drank her latte in a couple of gulps, shook the ice

around a little, and took the final sip. Her finger followed the spines of various books on architecture until she stumbled upon the first edition of *The Architecture of Charles W. Dickey/Hawaii and California.* Dickey was an architect she had admired. While flipping through it, a folded piece of parchment fell out onto the floor. Curious, Meg bent down to pick it up. She opened it and scribbled inside in elegant cursive handwriting was a note.

We are waiting for you. Yes, we mean YOU, Meg. 22.16 N 159.63 W.

She put her hand over her mouth. *What does it mean?* She didn't understand it. She pulled out her phone and immediately searched the longitude/latitude coordinates on the note. Google replied that the numbers were for the Napali coast of Hawaii on the rugged island of Kauai. She had always loved Hawaii, but had never been to Kauai. She and Mick had been on a vacation to Maui early in their marriage and ever since then she had dreamed about the mountains there. Intrigued, she stuck the note into the book and walked to the register.

As Bart rang her up, he admired the book. "Nice choice Meg. We just got this one in last week."

"Really?"

"Yeah, I didn't really get a chance to flip through it yet, but the cover spoke to me."

"Me too, Bart."

He studied her. "How are things Meg? You look tired."

"Oh, tell me about it, I am exhausted."

"You know, you got to get out more."

"I know, I know, it's just that work is always calling. I will."

"Sure. That will be $154.60."

Meg paid and left. Walking back to her car, using the newspaper as a shield against the rain again, she decided, that was it—she was going to take the next flight out of New York to Hawaii and find the author of the note and what it all meant.

Meg drove home, picked up the book and her Louis Vuitton purse and headed inside. She dropped the pink patterned Louis purse on the kitchen counter, grabbed a Perrier out of the fridge, and went over to her black leather Eames reading chair by the colossal courtyard window. Plopping down, she flipped the rare book open to the folded note again.

We are waiting for you. Yes, we mean YOU, Meg. 22.16 N 159.63 W.

She laughed. What did it mean? *Waiting for what?* She decided to call her friend Sally, an interior designer from the city. She dialed, and it rang a few times.

"Hey, Meg. Good to hear from you."

"Thanks."

"What's new?"

"Well, nothing much. Just working on that Manhattan gut and redo. God, what a bore!"

"Oh really? Well, how's it going?"

"Pretty good. Well, except for the fact that a $100,000 nineteenth-century Baccarat Crystal chandelier fell and crashed on the floor two weeks ago."

"Oh, my goodness! Are you serious?"

"Yes." She laughed. "Right after it landed, Mrs. Tolroy thought she was having a heart attack and had to go to the ER, but it turned out to be nothing more than a panic attack."

"Hey, a stiff gin martini and some deep breaths would have fixed that."

"Yeah, but who knew?" Meg looked at the note in her hand. "Hey, guess what?"

"What?"

"I found the strangest note in this book today at The Nook and Cranny."

"*Really? A note?* What did it say? Was it a love letter?"

Meg chuckled, "No, nothing like that. It just says, 'We are waiting for you. Yes, we mean YOU, Meg' and then has some longitude and latitude numbers."

"*What?* It has your name? That's crazy! And longitude-latitude...for where?"

"Somewhere in Hawaii."

"Oh, well, I would go there any day of the week, especially now that it's gray skies every day."

"Me too. But it spooked me out a little. This note."

"Hahaha, yeah me too. Don't worry about it. It's probably just a prank by some high school surf rats who know you hound that place. You're not going to go, are you?"

"I might." She laughed.

"Oh geez, well take your bug spray. I hear they have mosquitos the size of rats there."

"Better than this gloomy weather."

"I hear you. Hey, what's playing at the movies this weekend?"

"I don't know." Meg sighed. "I think I'm just going to take off. Do my own thing."

"Alright girl, well call me next time you're in the city. We'll go eat at Daniel. It's so posh."

"Sounds great! It's on me," Meg said.

"No way, I am not letting you pay *again*. You always pay."

"Alright, alright, we'll see. Love you girl. Ciao."

"Love you. Ciao."

Meg hung up and sat there staring at the wall. She looked out the expansive window to her right, watching the torrents of rain fall. She dialed Bob next, in Chelsea.

"Hi Meg."

"Hey Bob, let's say I was to take off for a week, could you manage the Tolroy project for me?"

"Sure, I guess so. I mean, why not?"

"Great, I need a vacation. I just have to escape this grey weather."

"I know what you mean. Where are you going?"

"I was thinking Hawaii. I'll send you the details soon. Ciao."

"Sounds good. Keep in touch. Bye Meg."

Meg hung up and called Mal and Peg, informing them about her plans. Then, she booked a round ticket to Kauai, to leave at nine in the morning from La Guardia airport and return the following week. Fortunately, she got the last remaining seat.

She packed her Ghurka leather shoulder carry-on bag with a week's worth of clothes that night and went to sleep with Hawaii on her mind—the ocean, the sun, the trade winds and the sound of tropical birds singing in the trees.

The next day it was gloomy, but not raining. A rideshare picked Meg up out in front of her condo at six am on the dot and drove her to New York La Guardia. When she got there, only a few people dotted the airport.

Breezing through check-in and security, Meg stopped by Starbucks to order an iced latte and a raisin bagel with cream cheese. She missed her two free-range boiled eggs, but a part of her felt a tad mischievous breaking routine. She had never done anything as wild as this before. She was actually following the trail of an obscure note left in a book. Her actions were so out of character, but that was also the thrill of it all.

Taking some deep breaths, she walked to her gate with her snacks and sat down to wait in the first-class lounge. She passed the time answering work questions from the end of the previous day. And in an hour, the plane began to board—Meg was first in line.

She settled into her first-class seat on the aisle. Being claustrophobic, the aisle seat was almost a requirement. Just the thought of crawling over someone to use the bathroom horrified Meg, even in the roomier first-class cabin.

A quiet Jewish man in a tweed blazer with curly brown hair, a hooked nose and wire-rimmed spectacles was reading what looked like a newspaper on his Kindle in the window seat. He acknowledged her with a nod and a smile. She had a seventeen-hour trip ahead of her with a layover in Minneapolis and Oahu, Hawaii.

After everyone boarded, the flight attendant asked Meg if she wanted a drink.

"Champagne, please."

Meg removed the book on Charles Dickey's architecture from her voluminous Kate Spade pink purse. Then, she flipped through it, studying the various houses.

When her champagne came, she sipped on it slowly, watching as the plane took off.

MEG LANDED in Lihue airport on the natural rugged island of Kauai at 5:59 pm on October 2nd, having slept through most of the long flight from Minnesota. Her neck and back were sore, but she barely noticed after watching the beautiful golden Hawaiian sunset through the airplane window as they made their final approach.

She loved first class because she got on and off the plane sooner—efficiency was the essence of life, she often said.

Carrying her Ghurka shoulder bag and her Kate Spade purse, she walked through the tropical airport to the ride share line. In a minute, she caught a Lyft in a Toyota Prius to the Cliffside Resort Hotel with a surfer with shoulder-length sun-bleached hair named Duke. She smiled when she saw his dashboard hula girl air freshener. She rolled her window down to feel the island breeze on her face. The freshness of the air made her feel like the mainland was a million miles away from this secluded slice of paradise. If she didn't find anything here, maybe she could at least find herself.

———

AT THE HOTEL, Meg checked in to her room and took a nightcap by the pool: a Blue Hawaiian cocktail (rum, blue curacao liquor, pineapple juice and coconut cream, garnished with a maraschino cherry and a pineapple wedge). Blazed tiki torches lit up the beach. The view of the waves crashing against the sandy shore was breathtaking.

Although she was exhausted from the long flight, the momentum of the trip filled her with anticipation. She checked the coordinates from her special note again on her phone via Google Earth. The land stretching over the address of the place, 152 Coconut Way, appeared to be some kind of sprawling estate right next to the ocean up the Napali coast. Meg's hotel was on the Napali coast as well, north of the area. There were structures dotting the 152 property, but when she zoomed in, the buildings were fuzzy.

Thrilled, she left her glass empty and went to the front desk, where she booked a car and driver to take her to the land at ten-thirty the next morning. Then, she went to her room, took a quick shower and crashed at eight pm.

That night, she dreamed that she was sitting on a high, barren rock cliff. Twenty feet of flat rock behind her, the cliff cascaded down to the ocean over fifty feet below. In front of her, facing the land in the distance, she balanced her feet on two small rocks, which felt unstable. Directly below her was a pool of clear water which stood between her and the land beyond. The water was brown, but she could see through it. There was large, flat rock below the surface, however it was deep enough for her to jump into and be safe. She knew in her heart the water was ice cold and the thought of that shocking temperature made her scared to jump. But there was no other way to get back to the land on the other side of the water below. She would have to leap off the rock into the water and swim to dry land. It would be a leap of faith, and when she hit the water, she would have to endure the cold shock of it for a moment. She thought about her money and purse and how she would have to leave them or else they would all get wet from the fall, and that frightened her too. Then, she awoke.

She shook the dream off, not knowing the meaning. She was jet-lagged as usual, but she was so excited by the day's possibilities that she bolted out of bed, took a shower, dressed in some gray linen pants and a white button-up starched shirt and headed down to a quick breakfast of Earl Grey tea, the freshest mango slices and two salted boiled eggs.

The driver, a Hawaiian named Earl, was waiting for her by his 2020 bright-yellow Ford Bronco Outer Shores Edition with the doors and top missing. He stood there like a chauffeur outside a limousine—donned in Hawaiian attire: a white-and-blue floral short-sleeved linen shirt, blue mirrored Ray Ban aviators, white linen pants and leather flip flops. After saluting Meg with a big "Aloha", he helped her into the passenger seat.

Once they exchanged pleasantries, Meg gave him the address and they drove over an hour through the winding Napali countryside—filled with evergreen mountains, bountiful coconut palms and lush grass the likes of which Meg had never seen, even in her short time in Maui.

They wound up a mountain where Earl came to a halt at a property line toward the top.

"This is it, my lady—152 Coconut Way. Do you want me to pull in the driveway?"

Meg looked out the open door of the Bronco nervously. A large teak gate, at least twenty feet tall, towered at the end of the crushed-shell drive.

"No, right here is fine. Thank you, Earl."

"No problem. Hey, here's my card if you want me to come pick you up later." He handed it to her, but she declined, saying she would find another way back. She didn't want to be constrained by any sort of obligation or timeframe. Besides, she had no idea what to expect.

"Wait, just a minute." Reaching into her wallet, she pulled out two twenty-dollar bills for his time, passing them to him.

"Mahalo."

Earl sped off, leaving Meg standing there on the side of the road, breathless.

She cautiously walked over to the driveway. When she stood in front of the teak gate, something strange happened—it started to magically open for her.

8

T hrough the now wide-open gate, Meg gazed down the long driveway. The crushed oyster shell drive continued in a straight path with giant palm trees planted along the sides. About a hundred feet ahead, the road curved to the right with a forest obscuring the view. Not knowing what to do, she decided to walk through the gate as if a hand was pushing her forward.

Walking down the road, the noise of the shells cracked beneath her feet, the ocean winds whistled through the trees and the sunlight scattered rays through the branches of the surrounding forest.

As she made her way, she had never felt so free. For the first time in her life, she was doing what her heart was willing her to do, not what her rational mind told her.

Rounding the curve, she saw a red Hawaiian-style barn up ahead, the road forking off on either side of it to the left and right. She kept walking and when she reached the barn, she looked down the path to the left, which moved downhill, disappearing into a green, densely forested area. Then, she looked to the right, where she saw a Spanish-style house about fifty feet up ahead.

Taking the path to the right, she glided down the road, her heart beating wildly with anticipation. She kept wondering *who* was here at these very specific geographic coordinates. *What was waiting for her? A certain feeling of familiarity surrounded her.*

When she reached the house, she was astounded to see what appeared to be a very old Romanesque building built completely out of the local stone (*Figure 2*). It had a strange vernacular appearance as well. However, the stone was exquisitely laid—the numerous arches and columns all correctly built in the Romanesque style. She had studied Romanesque buildings first-hand when she took a year off from Yale Architecture School to do a self-conducted study of the Spanish region of Andalusia, where she subsequently fell in love with the period and its stone buildings. This period lasted from the eighth to the fifteenth centuries and heavily influenced the Gothic era. But, what in the world was this building doing here in a tropical locale? It felt unknown, yet familiar.

At the front door, a gecko ran in front of her, stood on its hind legs and stared up at her. She grinned, leaned down and pet it under its chin. The little guy had a glimmer in his eye. Smiling, she straightened back up and was about to knock on the door when it suddenly swung open. And there in front of her stood an elegant Spanish gentleman about the age of sixty with serious eyes, the purest white hair slicked back, tanned skin and wire-rimmed glasses. "Good morning."

"Aloha, I am Meg."

"It took you long enough," he said with a Spanish accent. "Come on in!"

"Wait, you know me?"

"I sent for you...with the note. Of course I know you."

"Okay, but how did you know I would find you? I mean, from the note?"

"I kind of know these things." He smiled. "Come inside. Let's talk. I am Silas, by the way." He offered her his hand.

"Okay." She followed him inside, admiring the walls. "You must tell me about this building. I'm completely enamored with it."

"Yes, it is a very special building, and we are so fortunate to have it. Follow me, I will tell you everything you wish to know."

"Okay, great."

"They walked up a curved stair to the second floor and down the long hall to the sitting room where they sat down. A stone wall stood between them where two Medieval battle axes hung, crossing each other. Underneath them sat a curious red velvet foot stool.

Silas crossed his legs and brushed off his pants, then combed his beard.

"What do you want?" Meg asked reluctantly as her eyes traveled around the beautiful room.

"Ah, the age-old question. What do you want, Meg?"

"I don't like it when people answer questions with a question."

"Well, I don't either." He chuckled. "You see, I sent for you with the note because I am here and you were there. And I need you here now."

"Me? Why? What for?"

"You don't know this now Meg, but we know each other. I am Silas, the long-distance tutor on your architectural thesis, *Architecture: When Buildings Dance.* I always loved that title. Remember, we communicated by email. Your Prof. Bill Owens put you in touch with me."

"*Silas? Really?* But that was like a hundred years ago."

Silas laughed. "Yes, it was. Listen, I sent for you now because our community of like-minded people here at the Vortex has a mission to protect a very ancient Touchstone buried in a cave on this very property. This Touchstone emanates a very positive energy out to the whole world. Humanity's survival depends on it being protected." He paused, gauging her response. "The stone is how I knew you would come from the note and where to hide it. I have been working with its powers since I was a very small child. When I touch it, I gain insight."

"Okay, but what is it...this stone? And why do you need me again? I am just an architect. I don't know anything about such things."

"It's a stone with a blue gemstone core. It gives sight into the future, can restore health and lets us thrive here by filling this whole property and the world outside these walls with mana. Listen Meg," Silas said, leaning forward, his eyes stern. "I sent the note because we need an architect to design a huge building for the ages on our property here. And I knew when we worked together many years ago, you were that person."

"Okay, it sounds fascinating Silas. I will do it I guess, but I will have to work out of my office back in East Hampton. I can be in communication by phone and email. What's the pay?"

Silas leaned back, "Unfortunately, if you decide to accept the job, you would have to stay here, breathe the air, feel the wind, otherwise you won't get it. Money is no issue."

"I don't think so. I mean, how? I have a family you know, and a business. I have a life. I can't just move to Hawaii on a whim." There were many, many antique objects in the room that Meg simply could not ignore. "You have some beautiful furnishings."

He smiled. "Thank you. Why don't you think about it, while I give you a tour of our property and show you around?"

"Okay, sounds good. I mean, I booked my hotel for a week, so I might as well explore some while I am here."

He stood. "Alright, follow me. You will love it."

They walked out of the house towards the garden that stood

opposite the front door. Birds were chirping and the sun was bright, glistening off dew on the petals of flowers around them.

Meg noticed that the garden was both classical and tropical at the same time. There were clipped hedges and exotic flowers, plants and palm trees all carefully intermingled in an exotic way. There were even classical topiaries, but instead of animals like elephants and lions, these were of parrots, dolphins and monkeys.

"Like my handiwork?"

"You mean the topiaries? You did all these?!"

"Yes, I am the gardener as well as the Guardian here."

"Gosh, they're unlike anything I've ever seen before. They are so beautiful and perfect that they seem alive."

"Thank you, Meg."

In the middle sat an enormous round fountain that bubbled with an enchanting sound.

Silas and Meg kept walking. "On the right, you will see the Fountain of a Thousand Summers. One drop of its splendor will cure almost any ail." She stared pop-eyed at the circular fountain.

"What's it for? I mean, can I drink it?"

"Let's go have a cup of coffee at our old fort café (*Figure 3*). It's made with this wonderful water."

"Okay."

"Ciao guys," he said, as two forty-something women dressed in all white walked by.

"Aloha, Silas."

"Did you just say *ciao*? Only my mother and I say that."

Silas smiled, "You can call me mother if you like. If it would make you happy, that is."

She smiled, "Okay, Mom. I swear you don't look like her though." He laughed.

After making a path through a gravel walkway past the garden, they cut to the left down another way leading to a

Spanish-looking building. On the top of the second floor to the left was a covered porch where a few people, all dressed in white, were eating and talking.

They entered the downstairs, a big open room with various old black-and-white photos of Hawaiian landscapes hung along the walls. Some more men and women, all dressed in the same white, shuffled by.

In the entrance to the building, the pair took the stone stairs up into an open-air restaurant with a series of bistro tables covered in stark white tablecloths. A wide, polished teak bar sat on the back right wall. The two walked across the porch to a coffee bar built out of the same teak as the other bar. A Hawaiian man, built like an ox with the smoothest tan skin, greeted them.

"Aloha, Silas."

"Aloha, Kahuna, this is my friend Meg."

Meg said, "Hey."

"Aloha Meg."

"Do you like coffee?" Silas asked Meg.

"Of course, who doesn't?"

"Then you will love this, it's not just any coffee, it's fresh roasted, ground and brewed from green Kona beans from the Big Island of Hawaii. Many people still call that island Hawaii. It's a magical place too."

"So, what'll it be today Silas? Two coffees?"

"Yep."

"Coming right up, boss man."

After a few minutes of silence between them, the fresh coffee was delivered. The aroma won her senses, but noticing the lack of milk, she scoffed, "You drink it black? Ugh!"

"We drink it how it was always meant to be drunk. Taste it."

She took a sip, her eyes growing in amazement. "Wow, it's unbelievable really." She took another sip, scanning the people sitting on the porch. All of them dressed in the same boring white, she thought.

"Let's go down to the observation deck," Silas said.

"Ciao," he said to Kahuna, and walked ahead of Meg as she followed.

They cruised back past the main house to the right where over a dozen chickens were free range in the path ahead. As Silas approached, Meg observed they all miraculously filed into a line and bobbed off the path together in harmony. "Don't mind the moas, they are our wild chickens."

"Do they always move out of the way like that in perfect formation? That was weird."

"Ah yes, it's the Touchstone. I can ask them to move."

"How?"

"With my mind."

"Hahahaha, yeah right."

"You'll see. Believe me, there are stranger things than that here."

"I will believe it when I see it."

The two headed down a long, meandering trail that cut through the greenest forest Meg had ever seen. In the trees, she could hear the sounds of the jungle—monkeys and birds and the wind bristling through the trees. Then the brush cleared, revealing an observation deck. Walking to the rail, she saw waves crashing white water on a beautiful cove way down below the rocky, green-coated mountainous terrain.

"This is our home. Our mana. Feel it in the air we breathe, in the ground beneath our feet. This land is blessed by the Touchstone."

She looked out in awe, taking the dramatic view in.

"It's...it's beautiful."

He pointed down and over to the left. "That's where we will build it, deep in those trees; we will cut down the smallest number of trees necessary."

"The special building?"

"Yes, the one I want you to draw."

She put her hands on her hips, "Okay, okay, maybe so." The place was so pristine and untouched; she was warming up to the whole idea faster than she thought possible. "Why me again?"

He laughed. "We are the Guardians of the Touchstone. I have known you from a distance since the day you were born and have been preparing for this moment...the moment for you to draw this building. We live in harmony. We work in harmony." He walked over to her and placed both hands on her shoulders and said, "If you accept the job, the condition is to keep our address here at 152 secret, and to only leave once your work is done here. This place must be protected at all costs."

"How the heck have you known me since I was born?" Meg asked incredulously.

"It's the stone, I tell you. I see things in my visions when I touch it. And now, I have been working with it for so long, I see things all the time, even when I am not touching it. I have seen you since the day you were born."

"Really? But I am not special."

"Yes, but you see, that's just the thing. You are right person for the job. And the stone chose you. We are a community of people who are harnessing energy for the world's survival."

"Is the world in some danger?"

Silas looked at Meg. "What do you think?"

"Yeah, sometimes I think so. Sometimes, I think we are all mad, living in a mad world."

"In a crazy world, only the crazy people are normal, like that Japanese filmmaker guy said."

"Hahaha, I know what you mean." Meg paused, looking out over the land.

"Let me show you the stone, dear Meg. That will change your mind."

"Okay, thank you."

"Follow me."

Silas led and they hiked back past the main house, over to the far side of the road to the right of the barn where a tight trail disappeared into the green forest, heading up the mountain. They walked onto it. As it snaked this way and that, Meg could feel her legs burning as they climbed higher and higher into a thick cloud mist. Finally, the two reached a point where Silas turned to the left off the beaten trail and headed up a small hill. They were now surrounded by haze and standing at the opening of a dark cave with green moss growing all around the entrance. Without saying a word, Silas donned a headlamp from his pocket, turned it on and guided her into the hole. It was cool and damp inside, and in nothing more than a short walk they reached the illustrious stone, which began to emanate a soft white light and the same ethereal sound Fernando had heard so many years before. Meg stood beside it in awe, observing that the polished circular stone was about three feet tall with a one-foot radius, and the top where the light emanated seemed to be clear like glass, with layers of jagged blue gemstone in its core. Beside it was a worn-in low-slung bamboo chair with a canvas seat and back.

"What is it?" asked Meg.

"Touch it and find out for yourself."

Meg reached her right hand to it and touched the shimmering top. At that moment, she saw Hawaiian waterfalls rushing with the strongest water pierced by the brightest golden light she had ever seen, and the sound of the tropical birds echoed in her ears so clearly, it sounded like they were right there in the cave with them. Then she saw Silas in the vision, reaching out his hand with a tree growing in the center of his palm, and she knew it was the Tree of Life.

When the vision came to an end, Meg grasped Silas' forearm. "It was so real. So overwhelming. And you were there too."

"What you saw is for you and you alone, Meg. It will teach you in time. Let it marinate inside you. It will grow like a tree." He winked at her. Her eyes were sincere and alive.

"I think you've seen enough. Let's go back home."

He turned and started to walk out. She followed, still reeling from her experience.

Outside the cave, Silas smiled at her. "What do you think?"

"I think it's wonderful. I saw everything so clearly. I want to do it. To draw it."

"Great, I am glad to hear it."

"Can I at least call my family and tell them where I will be?"

"Okay, how about one call when we get back to the main house without revealing our address or my name and let that one soul be the messenger. Let's keep outside communication to an absolute minimum if possible."

"Okay..." She looked irritated.

"Look Meg, it must be simple like this, otherwise it won't work. Everyone will want to know where you are and come see you after a few months. Do this thing with us here. You'll be amazed how this place and deed can change you."

"Okay, I will do it. But I have to know the timeframe."

"3 months."

"Only 3 months? That's impossible."

"Not for us. We can do anything. You saw the stone. Now, when we reach the house, I will have Eight Foot call your hotel and cancel the rest of your stay. You can live here in the Tower of the main house. I have already prepared everything for you."

"Really? But how did you know I would stay?"

"I didn't...the stone told me."

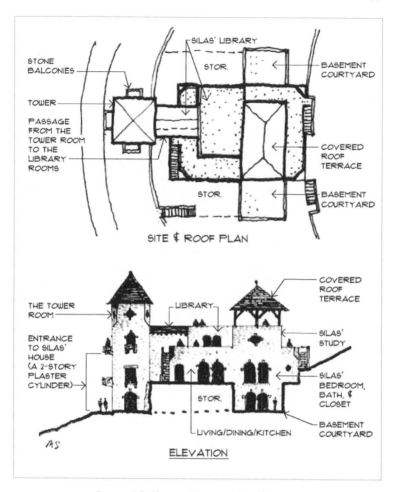

STONE BALCONIES

TOWER

PASSAGE FROM THE TOWER ROOM TO THE LIBRARY ROOMS

SILAS' LIBRARY

STOR.

BASEMENT COURTYARD

COVERED ROOF TERRACE

STOR.

BASEMENT COURTYARD

SITE & ROOF PLAN

THE TOWER ROOM

ENTRANCE TO SILAS' HOUSE (A 2-STORY PLASTER CYLINDER)

LIBRARY

COVERED ROOF TERRACE

SILAS' STUDY

SILAS' BEDROOM, BATH, & CLOSET

STOR.

LIVING/DINING/KITCHEN

BASEMENT COURTYARD

MS

ELEVATION

Figure 2 *Silas' house with tower where Meg stays*

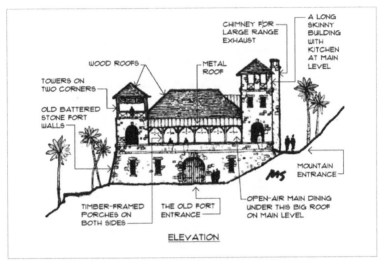

Figure 3 Old Fort Coffee Shop & Café

9

Meg followed Eight Foot up the curved stair to her room on the third floor of the Tower of the main house. The seven-foot-tall shirtless, barefoot, tattooed Samoan with a bald head who wore only white drawstring pants ducked under the doorframe to lead her in.

The room was an octagonal white room. Meg walked to the French doors. Outside, a jungle of forest ran all the way down the jagged lush mountain slope to the blue ocean in the distance. Every wall of the eight-sided room had the same circular windows at least fifteen feet above the floor and three pairs of French doors she could look out. She walked over to one of the French doors opposite the bed and gazed out over the fabulous garden with row after row of exquisitely cut topiaries, some in the shape of birds and animals: monkeys, gorillas, a toucan and a rhino.

She checked out the bathroom, which had white walls with white tile floors and a white claw-foot tub—the kind she wished she had in her condo because it reminded her of her paternal grandmother Dot's house in Newport.

When she came out, she asked, "What about my clothes, big guy?"

A man of few words, Eight Foot spoke, "Your bags will be delivered to us by hotel courier soon. But you might want to dress like us." With his hand, he offered her the closet to the left of the door. She swung the bamboo-shuttered doors open to reveal a lineup of the same green outfit. They looked just like scrubs, except finer cotton and more tailored.

"What, am I a turtle or something? I thought we only wore white here. Are you tricking me?"

"Green is the color of hope. You can draw in this. It will help you."

"Okay, I guess."

"And look, Silas made arrangements for you to have a drafting table up here with tracing paper, pens and pencils." She walked over, caressing the newly placed table with her hand. "I will bring you some food. There's a special movie tonight at the Field of a Thousand Hopes."

"How nice, where is that?" Meg said.

"On the other side of the garden. Be back soon." Eight Foot left.

Meg emptied her pockets and saw the note that brought her there. Smiling, she opened the bedside table drawer and placed it there for safekeeping.

Now that she was alone, she had time to study the architecture of the space. She realized that the stone tower was a square on the outside, but that it had a smooth plaster cylinder on the inside wall for the circular stair below her room. There was also a smaller octagonal room for the room she was in. The closet and bathroom were in the space between the square and the octagon. It occurred to her that it was a non-modernist, non-linear, Eastern notion of layering different shapes within each other. Intrigued by this, she wanted to know more.

She took a long shower. The water was the cleanest, most surreal water she had ever bathed in, and she wondered if it might be the same water from the fountain.

When Meg got out, she slipped into her green garb and noticed there was a plate of fresh tropical fruit—the likes of which she had never seen before—waiting for her on the vintage bamboo bedside table, along with a coconut with a straw stuck in it. Grapes, the bluest blueberries, dragon fruit, durian, diced pineapple, mango slices and jackfruit adorned the plate, and a jar of coconut cream was whipped up with some honey to go on top of it all. In a small vase on the dinner tray was a single white plumeria flower, the floral symbol of birth and love.

She ate all the fruits and coconut cream she could until she was full, then she picked up the flower and waltzed to the bathroom mirror where she tucked it behind her ear like the Hawaiian luau girls did. "Perfect!"

She decided to explore the Library immediately on the 3rd floor of Silas' house right next to her room.

She first entered a small hallway and then saw the doors, which were hand-carved mahogany ones from India that opened onto a sprawling hand-woven oriental rug. The room, filled with rare editions and out-of-print books on every subject imaginable, completely surpassed The Nook and Cranny— being more like Argosy in Midtown Manhattan. Founded in 1925, Argosy was a treasure trove of antiquarian books; however, the truth was, this library even *beat the best of Manhattan*. Meg almost cried when she smelled that familiar antique aroma of a bygone area when people still read for knowledge, and not solely to be entertained, emanating from the pages collected on the shelves. Meg poked around some more and realized that there were at least two or three more of these book rooms, but she suddenly felt that she had to get back to her room.

As soon as she did, there was a knock on the door. She opened it to Eight Foot, who politely handed her the Ghurka bag from her hotel. She thanked him and he left.

fter an hour, Meg was reading Henry Miller's *Stand
Still Like the Hummingbird* in her bed when a loud
rapping came at the door. She opened it to Silas, who
was smiling.

"You look marvelous!"

"Awww, thank you Silas.

I think the green suits me, kind of like the flower and this
place."

He chuckled, "I think so too. I want to show you the site
now."

"The site? Really? Cool."

"Follow me."

"Okay, can't wait!"

The two walked downstairs where they climbed onto a
camouflage-patterned ATV four-wheeler and headed along a
paved road past the right of the Hawaiian-style hardwood barn.
Silas snaked his way down the mountain through forested
greenery for about five minutes until they finally came to the
land for the palace.

A canopy of lush trees surrounded a clearing on a large

spread of land and the mountain facing the ocean jutted up in
the background, trees dotting it. Just through the jungle, there
was a cylindrical view of the ocean a hundred feet away below
the mountain cliff.

Silas parked the ATV. "Well, this is it!"

"It looks even better at close range."

"Yes, I do say so! You ready to walk the grounds?" He turned
to her.

"Sure, let's do it."

Silas got off and Meg followed.

"My dream is for the building to climb the mountain in the
grandest scale, with domes and towers." He pointed up at the
mountain. "A building fit for a queen."

"Domes and towers?" Meg thought about her last fantasy
drawing the day she found the note. "Who's it for?"

"Everyone here. The point is for you to imagine it, the way
you always do Meg."

"Okay, but what's it for? I mean, is it a house or a center of
worship for your community?"

"It's a building for our community. A house for you and me
and everyone else here."

"Okay," she said as she walked around, studying the
grounds. "It's amazing, there is all this energy coming from the
ground, I feel so alive here. Is it the Touchstone?"

"Of course." They walked the flat grounds below the hill
together, eventually coming upon two humble gravestones. "A
long time ago, many hundreds of years past, two special people
to me were buried here." He paused, studying the graves with
his hands on his hips. "Now, do let me tell you our story."

"Okay, please do."

"When the Spanish first set foot on Kauai in the sixteenth
century, they were enthralled by it. One of their crew members
was a stone mason named Simón Córdoba who had previously
worked on late Spanish/Moorish churches in the Andalusia

region of Spain that had Moorish influences. The natives were friendly and hospitable, so Simón and his brother Juan decided to stay on this beautiful slice of paradise, where they lived among the natives.

"After some time, the *hermanos* built themselves two houses with the local stone. Later they built even more buildings for storage purposes. Their craft and expertise in late Spanish/Moorish stone architecture allowed them to design and construct stone barrel vaults and domes that the natives had never seen. Those are the houses on our main property; even my house and the Tower where you are staying was built by the hands of these men.

"In time, they fell in love with a pair of beautiful native women and became an integral part of the community. They taught the locals to lay the stone vaults, so they were able to build bigger structures together—one such building being a large congregation hall we use for celebrations on the other side of the property. Simón and Juan died a tragic death by falling off a hiking trail that gave way under their feet on the north side of the island.

"Their wives were so distraught by their passing, they cast the community away from the land and lived like hermits until the end of their days, when they died in peace. Having no heirs of their own, the small stone compound was eventually left abandoned and completely covered with vines—hidden from view until a Spanish adventurer named Fernando discovered it. He made a claim to the land and hundreds of acres around it. A humble man from Granada, Spain, Fernando's hero was Juan Ponce de Leon—the fifteenth-century Spanish explorer—and he had set off to explore the world like his hero.

"But one day, as luck would have it, he found the Touchstone hidden in one of the caves and started sitting with it, placing his hand on it. He began to look and feel younger, and suddenly, he could communicate with the wind, trees and animals. While sitting there, he also saw into the future some-times. That man was my father."

Meg looked amazed. "Really?"

"Yes." Silas paced a little, thinking. "Over time, he hired the local villagers to help him clean up the island and start developing it by planting beautiful local species around the property. Then, he met and fell in love with my mother, a beautiful Hawaiian angel named Kala. Aw, you would have loved her Meg. She was a short thing, but what a fighter and strong as the wind. Unfortunately, my parents lost their lives when I was only ten in an automobile accident. I, then, inherited the whole estate when they died. We wanted them buried on the land here, for this spot was so special to them."

"That's a truly amazing story. So lucky that you were born here."

"What about you?"

"What do you mean?"

"Well, this place, is it right for you?"

"I think so. I feel good here; I mean, I want to be here now."

"What else do you want to know, dear Meg?"

"Nothing right now." At that, she began traversing all over the mountainous terrain, getting a feel for the land and how and where the house should be.

After a little time, Silas spoke. "When you are done looking, I have something special to show you Meg."

"Okay, great."

IN A BIT, Meg came over to him and Silas motioned her to follow him along the flat property to the southern tip of it, where a small stone square building with a door that headed into the mountain was waiting. He typed in a code on the keypad, the door slid open, and they walked in. Next, they were standing in an industrial-looking, stainless-steel elevator. Silas hit the bottom of two buttons, the door closed, and the elevator glided down.

When it stopped, they exited and walked down a long, cavernous hall. The space had natural mountainous walls, which cooled the interior space.

At the end of the hall, the pair entered a quaint circular room with comfortable teak chairs with squishy black cushions, an earthen fireplace and a round table in the center. "This is our lounge room," Silas explained. "And this long hall leads out to the ocean."

"Oh, I just love the ocean. Take me there, please."

"Sure." He walked and she followed him down the stone hall, which went on and on for an eternity until it opened onto a secluded beach cove with rocky cliffs towering on either side of it, shooting up to the sky.

"This is all ours. Look at this beautiful golden Kauaian sand." He smiled. "Of course, all beaches in Hawaii are open to the public, but no one ever stops here. Why would they? It's small and can only be reached by boat."

Meg walked out, slipped her shoes off and scrunched her toes up in the sand. Then she felt the saltwater with her hands and breathed the fresh ocean air deep into her lungs.

"I miss the sun and the beach so much. I never go anymore since what happened between my ex-husband and my sister. Or do you know about that also?"

Silas smiled. "I know a lot of things. Some important and some less. That seems to be off my radar."

"Yeah," she said, squinting her eyes out towards the ocean. "The ocean is a trillion constellations of water drops, like stars in the galaxy. The tide flows in and out, never ceasing, never stopping to think, 'What if I don't go to the shore today? What then?' Sailors use boats to travel across it, but they know in their hearts they can never tame it. Taming the sea would be like taming the wind. It's bigger than us. It follows its own rules.

Lives by its own time and fills the four corners of the earth with hope that somewhere out there, paradise lies waiting for us all. The mighty fish found in its belly feed us and its shores wash us clean from a day's troubles. How many oysters have settled a night's fight between quarrelers? Or brought lovers together?"

"That's very poetic Meg. Do you want some oysters?" Silas smiled with a twinkle in his eye.

"Maybe," she said, smiling at him. And he laughed.

After a while, the two left the beach and headed back up the elevator to the main compound. Silas invited her to the movie at the Field of a Thousand Hopes and she obliged.

PAST THE GARDEN sat a long rectangular field with manicured grass and sixteen white folding chairs in two rows of eight set up along it. At the front was an expansive white screen. Most of the chairs were filled, the audience chatting quietly.

Silas led Meg to the area and, shy as usual, she took a seat in the back. Silas continued on to the front where he addressed the assembly: "Now everyone, our movie tonight is the video of our Touchstone, emanating healing frequencies in the form of sound. Just relax and behold what the Field of a Thousand Hopes has in store for us this evening."

Silas sat down in the front, while Kahuna flipped the switch on the projector. The video showed the Touchstone emanating the most beautiful blue and white light from its core, while an incredible sound different than the one Meg heard earlier came from within its belly. It was beautiful, almost angelic.

When the movie ended after forty-five minutes, everyone clapped.

"Woohoo!" Kahuna yelled.

"I love that sound," Meg commented. "And I feel better, too."

A young woman named Violet sitting next to her with a bob haircut and blue eyes said, "The sound is designed to repair the body at a cellular level. The Touchstone can do that. It's amazing, isn't it?"

"Yes, truly."

11

1901

Fernando woke in the cool, dark cave, sensing danger all around him. He turned his face from side to side, but couldn't see anything in the pitch-black cavern. His neck throbbed with pain. What had happened? He remembered that he had blacked out just as he touched the strange stone to his left. He reached over with his fingers and could feel its body. Still warm, it was vibrating an energy from its core.

Fernando sensed a man approaching from behind him in the cave; he could hear his footsteps. He pulled his navaja blade from his pocket as quietly as he could. Playing dead with the weapon clenched firmly in his right hand, he waited until the steps grew nearer. When he could hear the man's breath, he turned on the ground and sprung up as fast as he could, holding the blade out in front of him.

He couldn't see anything, but he was surrounded by hate. He could feel it in his bones.

At that moment, the man tackled him to the ground and, straddling him, began to punch at his face. Fernando's first instinct was to stab him, so he struck deep at where he imagined the man's jugular would be amidst the swinging fists. The strike hit, and the man belted out in excruciating pain, then fell off him to the side. Hustling to his feet, Fernando ran out of the cave as fast as he could, making his way back down the mountain to his satchel, then home.

When he returned to his house, his Hawaiian wife Kala was nursing their newborn child, Diego. Fernando stormed in, grabbed his rifle, loaded it and sat down on the living room sofa, a small amount of blood trickling down his forehead, knees shaking as he told his wife what he had seen.

In sheer terror, Kala ran with their baby into the Tower bedroom and locked the door to hide, in case the dangerous fellow or his friends came to the main house to rob them.

After a few days holding down the fort, Fernando decided the man must have died in the cave. So, he took a team of his four most trustworthy men to go and inspect the cave.

At the entrance, there was a trail of blood going off to the left of the cave's mouth, where it disappeared over the hill. Fernando's right-hand man, Ahe, followed it.

In a minute, he yelled from past the hill, "Over here, my friend!"

Fernando and the other men followed his voice until they reached the body of a dangerous-looking bald Spaniard dressed in military fatigues, the navaja knife still stuck in his neck—his eyes rolled back into his head.

"Who is he?" Fernando asked.

Ahe checked the man's body for identification, but he wasn't carrying any. "I don't know. Let's give him a proper burial though," Ahe said.

"I don't know that he deserves it, he almost killed me in that cave," Fernando said, wiping the sweat from his brow and cleaning the morning fog off his glasses with his shirt.

"Everyone deserves it. That's what I believe," Ahe said.

"I guess so, okay you guys," Fernando addressed the group, "let's take his body down the mountain and bury him away from our homes. And don't tell anyone we know about this. He could have friends. And not the kind we want to deal with."

The group picked the man up, who was quite the weight, and carried him down the mountain.

After burying him on the far side of the property in an unmarked grave, Fernando returned to his family and took a short lunch of *lau lau*—a Hawaiian dish of steamed fish and pork wrapped in *taro* leaves and a *ti* leaf—and a cup of kava kava to calm his nerves.

The next day, Fernando decided he would explore the cave again now that the man was gone. The long, arduous walk back up the mountain caused Fernando to fear another strange encounter might occur in the blackness of the cave. But as he walked up the path, he heard that same angelic sound again. This time it was different, more beautiful and seraphic.

Hiking up the mountain, his heart was beating fast with fear. He was scared he might die or black out again, but the music was now filling him with peace. Reaching the cave, he entered slowly, and the ethereal light emanated from the stone again as he approached it. Standing before it, he was now very drawn to placing his hand on it again, even though doing so had almost killed him. But this time, something reassured him it would be okay.

With his hand shaking, Fernando touched the top of the polished stone again and entered a deep trance, where he saw green mountains rushing with the cleanest water and his newborn son, as an older gentleman, working with a team of animals on a stone building that was the most exquisite creation. And, in a moment, the vision ended just as fast as it had come.

12

That night in his reading room, Silas was reflecting on the day's events. His long, tanned fingers spread out over his knees as he sat. Quiet, funny and reserved, he was overjoyed that Meg was home. That was how he thought about it anyhow. He was Fernando's only son, inheriting the property and a gold mine located in one of its caves at the age of ten, when his father and mother died tragically in a car accident. One hundred and twenty years of Silas' life had passed by on this sacred land his father had named the Vortex. The Touchstone ensured that Silas never seemed to age much at all, and he looked a mere sixty to most folks. Fernando had taught Silas how to sit with the stone and feel its energy, using its power to learn and grow.

From his life as a boy there, he saw things in a special way —always looking beyond the surface. At an early age, after working with the stone, he learned how to communicate with the animals and trees on the property, and the winds, too. And over time, he had mastered how to control them. That was when he changed his name from Diego to Silas, which meant "Man of the Woods".

One day, when he was fifteen, he saw Meg and the building of the palace along the coast in a vision. He also had the most vivid dreams. He had even seen Meg in his dreams and waking states every day for the last hundred years. He had waited and waited for her—even going looking for her once in Miami, where he had seen her in a vision from the stone, but he had never found her. The stone was like that sometimes. Much of what it predicted came to be, but other things were a mere foreshadowing of events that could change inexplicably before they happened.

He was sworn to secrecy about the Vortex's land by his father—no one could ever know about the magic contained within it. Most of the members of the community drifted to the Vortex from a dream of their own, or came to know Silas by some odd coincidence, or a *coincidance*, as he liked to call it—because meaningful "accidents" really did happen kind of like a dance.

One day, he was on the beach relaxing when he saw Mickey, a blond-haired surfer dude, swimming madly to the shore. Silas lifted his Persol sunglasses and squinted to see who it was. When Mickey beached on the shore of the Vortex, he explained to Silas how he was kayaking around the island when his kayak began taking on water through a slight crack he didn't know about in the hull, and it sank about a hundred yards off the shore.

Silas handed him a towel and warmed him by a fire in the earthen fireplace of the cave room, where they shared some fresh durian and a coconut. They talked about the community a bit. Silas asked Mickey about his life and the young man shuddered at the thought of his past.

"My life?" he asked.

"Yes, tell me who you are."

Then the blonde surfer proceeded to tell his life story. How he was born in Ohio, abandoned behind an old dumpster at a

Walgreens when he was ten years old. And how by eleven, he was forced into a foster home with raging alcoholic parents. All he had ever known growing up was violence. "It was sad really," Mickey added.

Then Silas said, "I know about the cat."

"*The cat?* I mean *you know?*"

"Yes, I know about ole Elvis and how you threw him off the roof of the building."

"*Really?* But how? I mean, you know that? No one knows about that, not even my parents."

"Yes, well, he didn't die, you know. You thought you killed him, but after he hobbled off, he was rescued by a young couple and nursed back to health."

Mickey just sat there speechless. "Tell me who you are, mister. I mean I want to know. How do you know that?"

"There is a magical Touchstone hidden on our sacred property here. It has powers. It shows me things about life and people. I am assembling a group here to guard it."

"Really? Tell me more, brother. I got to know."

Silas told Mickey about his family and the stone and how it protected the world from evil. This touched Mickey's heart and he informed Silas he never wanted to leave. Silas agreed, and the rest was history. All the members had arrived in a similar fashion, many with little family of much consequence.

13

M eg's mother Scarlett had received the strange call earlier that day from Meg, who told her she was going to be staying on an island in Hawaii to design a very unusual building for an eccentric man for a few months, and she needed complete privacy. Meg had instructed her for the time being to inform the office about the assignment, giving Bob full authority to run things. When Scarlett asked her for the address and details, Meg told her she couldn't say.

Meg's mother and her sister, Dawn, sat on the front porch of Meg's childhood shingle-style home in Newport, Rhode Island. Built in the 1880s, the house had been an endless source of inspiration for Meg growing up, as she crawled the wood floors and wandered all over its many rooms. In fact, the whole town of Newport had inspired her with its beautiful historic homes.

The two ladies lounged in white wicker chairs sipping their Earl Grey tea with milk from Scarlett's fine china in the cold Newport weather, staring out at the frigid gray Atlantic rolling in the distance. Dawn had a Hermes scarf thrown over her lilac-blue J. Crew toggle coat. A stunning blonde with the fullest lips anyone had ever seen, Dawn's beauty surpassed both Scarlett's and Meg's. It was the main thing that had drawn Meg's ex-husband, Mick, to her.

The two were discussing the dismal possibility that Meg had been kidnapped—her call being nothing more than a forced act by an assailant. Dawn breathed in the cold air blowing off the Atlantic and sighed.

"What happened to her? I just don't understand it. This is so not like her. I mean, we haven't spoken since Mick, but I am still so worried about her. It wasn't my decision to stop talking."

"Me too. What a weird call. I truly hope she is okay."

"I know. If she isn't, I'll feel so bad about it because of the situation between us. I mean, when was the last time we spoke? It's been over a year now."

"Well, you shouldn't have done what you did. That's why, darling."

"I know, I feel just awful about it."

The two sat in silence for a moment when Meg's father James walked out, not knowing what the two were discussing.

"Hey girls, want some New England clam chowder? My specialty. I just threw some logs on the fire and its nice and toasty inside."

"Alright Pop, be in in a sec."

Sensing the sadness, James came closer. He was wearing a V-neck hunter-green cashmere sweater and stonewashed blue jeans. He had a bushy brown mustache and well-groomed hair. "Hey girls, I know how worried you must be about Meg. Hopefully it's just a favor for some eccentric client. Come inside, you'll feel better by the warmth of the fire."

"Thanks Dad. Let's go in, Mom."

"Okay baby."

The two walked inside carrying their teas. The house was decorated in a Sister Parish New England style with chintz slipcovers, early twentieth-century paintings and continental antiques that smelled of oiled wood. They sat in the living room by the crackling fire while James served them two serious bowls of chowder. Everyone said James made the best New England clam chowder anyone had ever tasted—unless one had been to the Scraggly Oar on Nantucket Island, from where James had heisted the recipe during a summer job there as a line cook in his teenage days.

"I think it's going to snow this weekend," James said.

"Oh nice, that would be excellent," Dawn said, stirring her soup. "Dad, do you think that Meg will ever forgive me after what happened with Mick?"

James took a seat on the tufted leather sofa facing them, crossed his legs and took a bite of his clam chowder.

"She may never let it go sweetheart. You broke her heart."

"But it's just so not fair, I mean, we're sisters. I can't change the past."

"I know dear. I never liked him anyway, but it was wrong what you did. Meg loved him. What can I say? Enjoy your chowder; it will take your mind off this whole thing for now."

"Yeah, you're right." She stirred the chowder again. "I never loved him, you know. That's for sure. He never loved me, either. In fact, he has never loved anyone except himself. He seduced me."

BACK IN EAST HAMPTON, as the day crawled on, Sam and Peg had started to get worried about Meg after her mother's bizarre call. Mal continued working in a stew of self-hate, oblivious to the whole thing.

Punctual to a tee, Meg never missed a day of work, so it truly alarmed the office that she would just leave the whole operation on the string of her mother's command. Although

Bob had been cordial with Scarlett when she called him, he was now questioning the whole thing.

Sam rang Meg's cell endlessly and sent text after text. Having received no reply, he decided to call the police to talk with an officer about Meg's strange message.

While waiting for the police to arrive, Sam asked Peg, "What are we going to do if she doesn't come back and just leaves us here under Bob's command for three months? It's crazy!"

"Not sure honey, but the cop is here," Peg said, seeing the Hampton's finest knocking on the door. By this point, Mal had emerged from the back and was leaning on the secretarial wooden cubicle, listening to what was going on.

"I can't believe Meg has gone missing. All of this, and I am leaving for the Testicle Festival in Florida tomorrow!" Sam announced.

"Well, it will just have to wait, Sam," Peg said as she opened the door for Officer Henry.

He entered. "Howdy folks, did somebody call about a missing person?"

"I wish, somebody kidnapped our sweet little ole Meg," Sam said, watching the officer with delight.

The officer, a square-faced macho guy, wore a black leather jacket and brimmed police hat. He flipped his notepad open and started to write everything down.

"When did you see her last?"

"Yesterday, she left early," Sam answered.

"What was she wearing?"

"Oh, I don't know," Sam said.

"Have you seen her since?"

"No, we just got this one bizarre call with instructions for us through her mother, Scarlett," Sam said.

"Okay, did she leave an address?"

"No."

"Well, I am going to need to try to reach her and get a list of her closest contacts to do a full report on this."

Peg rattled off Meg's phone number and her family and friends' names and numbers from the rolodex to Henry as he jotted them down, then left.

Mal commented, "This is just so strange—Meg of all people. Miss Orderly."

"I know, I would trade places with her if I could, our dear Meg. Love her to death," Sam said.

14

The next morning was Sunday, October 3rd.

Meg had a night of the most wonderful sleep, full of mystical dreams. When she awoke, she grabbed her pens and pad and walked down the Tower stairs back through the illustrious garden, where a group led by Silas was performing the morning Pa Tuan Chin Qi-Gong movements, finally arriving at the building where the fresh coffee was served. She kept thinking about that cup she had yesterday.

"Aloha Meg," Kahuna said.

"Aloha Kahuna, three shots of espresso, black."

"You got it. I can feel the winds today, they are majestic," Kahuna said.

"Me too. I love that island breeze."

Kahuna served her the espresso in a triple shot glass and grinned.

"Thanks so much," she said, taking it.

"Anytime."

She downed the black coffee and headed over to find a table in the shade.

Before drawing, she stared off into the surrounding jungle on the other side of the building for a moment.

Closing her eyes, she imagined the structure first in her mind. It was always that way. She dreamed every building into being in her mind, and then she drew it.

When Meg finally started sketching, she intentionally drew more fluid shapes scattered around on paper, allowing a bit of automatic drawing to occur from her subconscious mind— something she learned from her Jungian studies and through trial and error, as well as lots of practicing and "allowing".

She began to build onto the amorphic shapes more geometric forms of the house she had already started drawing back at the Saltbox the day before she left for Hawaii. These forms, in her mind, were mostly archetypal geometries, but they allowed her to "see" and formulate on paper a hierarchy for them and a kind of relationship from one form to the next, the most important being the Theater building.

The Theater, a large gathering space for all of the members of the community, could become a catalyst for the other buildings to reference and *communicate* with. In Meg's mind, all buildings spoke in one form or another through a kind of geometric vibration. One saw this most clearly in hillside villages in Italy and Greece, and in African villages where there were real semblances between each building.

Meg knew these things through her readings at first, and then via direct observation and intuitive understanding. She had often applied these principles in her work to varying degrees, but never to this extent.

Now she could understand all those years of sketching and dreaming of structures and architectonic shapes. And she sensed that this was her destiny. Her inner voice was truly starting to communicate more clearly with her outer self.

Perhaps because she now had no worries in the world but to think about this one single building—this *living* thing. Meg had also come to know through her studies and observations that all things on earth had *anima mundi*—a spirit within them, whether they were a rock or a chair. She harnessed this active spirit in her design in order to enhance the principle to its fullest capacity.

Once Meg had blocked out these archetypal shapes on paper, she went back to the site with Silas the next day—the place where the magic would happen—so that she could *feel* the energy of each area for every building form (*Figure 4*).

She walked to the site and measured by steps the rough dimensions for each building based on her sketches. Then she sat for some time *inside* each form, feeling the earth's energy and visualizing the interior spaces for each one—a practice she had started early in her career, gradually developing it into a fine art of perception and visualizing forms, spaces, volumes, light and shadow, and so on. She was aware that these images were not from herself, but from a higher reality that she simply had to get in touch with, and here on this island, on this mountain and this spot of land, all of her practice and work was paying off. This would be her *opus magnum*. Her life's work.

Sketching once again, Meg started producing a figure-ground drawing, with the buildings being the *figure* and the spaces between being the *ground* (*Figure 5*).

She had studied the importance of the figure-ground relationship in her readings on Gestalt therapy, as well as in graphic design classes in college. Later she used these ideas in her architectural designs at Yale. In this case, the ground areas would be developed as courtyard gardens. All of the buildings would have these courtyards, which in turn would connect each building to the next. Each courtyard would have fountains and flowering vines and plants. The building would scale up into the mountain just like Silas wanted.

Meg had also discovered from her travels to Spain, and especially to the Alhambra in Granada, that human beings thrived in the presence of the sound of running water and the wonderful fragrances of flowers. Some of the courtyards would have runnels of water that continued into other courtyards. These represented the flow of life.

She eventually drew out about eleven buildings and seven courtyards, which allowed her to think about the physical as well as the psychological relationships between them all. She did not want to draw up every building in detail at this point— she just wanted enough to see where the design was going.

Figure 4 *Meg's first rough sketch of the palace*

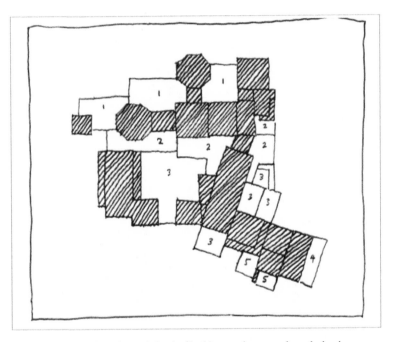

Figure 5 *Figure/ground sketch of buildings and courtyards, and 5 level
changes, 1 being the highest*

15

A t midday on Monday, Silas came over to check on Meg while she was finalizing the initial sketch at the café. Placing a hand on her shoulder, he asked, "What are you working on today, my dear Meg?"

"Oh, just the drawing. I think I have it already."

"Already? Wow, let me see."

"It's just the initial sketch. Here you go." (*Figure 6*). Meg tilted the drawing towards his eye.

Studying it, Silas commented, "Brilliant! It's an absolute masterpiece. Both magical and mysterious. I was ninety-nine percent certain before, but now I know without a doubt that you are the one to bring this building into being. By the way, why are these buildings on the end at a different angle?"

"Well, they follow the mountain and its slopes and contours."

"That is a beautiful idea. I love how the buildings seem to be organic in their relationship to the mountain."

"Thank you, I'm still working it out in my mind. It takes time, you know. But my vision is that it is built out of solid stone with all these domes and interior courtyards and pools, and it even scales up into the mountain."

"Well, it looks like paradise, that's what I think Meg. And a name comes to mind. *Ha'alulu Maika'i.* It means 'good vibration' in Hawaiian."

"Well, I wouldn't go that far, but thanks anyway. I like the name though."

"You underestimate yourself. Time will tell."

"I was wondering, who are my builders? My building has to be built by the best artisans and craftsmen. You know everything we use in my work is real, authentic, no substitutes. How are we going to swing that here if you don't want a big outside team coming in?"

"Well, I wouldn't have it any other way, Meg. Of course it will be real. We have the best craftsmen available in our own community. They all live on the island. I informed them about our project, and they are all waiting on you."

"Oh, wonderful! All that for little ole me."

Silas chuckled. "Of course. Anything for our master architect."

LATER THAT AFTERNOON, lying on her comfortable bed in the Tower, Meg dozed off into a magical dream about *Ha'alulu Maika'i.*

In the dream, she was wandering through exotic courtyards with the most amazing fragrances and sounds, as well as astonishing stone buildings in the most wondrous compositions. There were domes, glorious colonnades and loggias of such variety and scale that she began to weep—they were like her fantasy drawings, but now she was inside their walls. And it was as though she had been channeling these buildings all along, for the moment when this day would come.

Next, she was standing in a large octagonal room, a theater of some sort, with an enormous stone dome. Suspended from the dome were hundreds of candles on numerous fanciful chandeliers hanging at different levels. The flickering candlelight and the shadows on the walls and dome were the most magical thing she had ever beheld in a building, equaled only by being in Istanbul's Hagia Sophia at night.

Then she was in a tower, looking out over a vast paradise, a lush utopia of buildings and gardens like she had never seen or experienced before. Everything was vibrating with its own energy—the colors more vivid, the buildings more alive than her waking reality.

Meg awoke with a clarity of purpose about the house. She knew what she had to do, but first she quickly made sketches of images from her dream that were still vivid in her memory (*Figures 7, 8 & 9*).

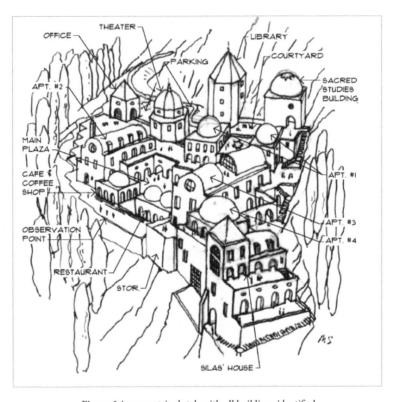

Figure 6 *Axonometric sketch with all buildings identified*

Figure 7 *Meg's dream about* Ha'alulu Maika'i, *1st sketch*

Figure 8 *Meg's dream about* Ha'alulu Maika'i, *2nd sketch*

Figure 9 *Meg's dream about* Ha'alulu Maika'i - *3rd sketch*

16

It was dusk when Meg rose and looked out the window, where she saw tiki torches aglow lining the edge of the field on both sides in the distance past the garden. Some groups dressed in white gathered together, waiting for the luau.

She grinned, fixed her hair in the bathroom mirror and headed down the Tower stairs. What a relief to not have to figure out what clothes to wear, she thought, admiring her green threads. She felt guilty about feeling so free and happy about being at this place. After all, she was the girl who never missed work, and was always on time.

Outside, the Hawaiian brown mutt dog named Biscuit who lived on raw meat scraps and bones greeted her, following her through the garden, the moonlight a shimmering dazzle of white reflecting off the surface of the fountain. When the smell of the roasting kalua pig hit her nose, Biscuit rushed forward past her to get his share.

Chloe, a cute blonde woman in her twenties with amber eyes and a grass hula skirt on, greeted Meg with a seashell lei, which she placed over Meg's neck.

"Aloha Meg, so glad you joined us here tonight for the luau. I'm Chloe."

"Thank you, I'm glad to be here. These shells are so beautiful. Where did you get them?" she said, her fingers touching the hot pink and black shells.

"Ah yes, these are Ni'ahu shells from the Forbidden Island. Very special."

"Interesting, am I forbidden?"

Chloe laughed, "Stop it girl, everyone who makes it here is meant to be here, even you."

"Thank you, I think." She took a deep breath and exhaled. She was nervous... or was she excited? She didn't know, but needed to find out. Maybe a mixture of both. She walked over to Kahuna and Silas who stood by the pig, which was being cooked in the ground and covered with huge banana leaves. Her heart was truly warming to Silas, who looked so good tonight.

"Welcome Meg," he said, smiling at her. Dressed in his customary all-white garb, he also wore a special necklace of white beads—not a lei, but something else. Silas thought about explaining the meaning of the adornment to her, but decided not to. It would be too much for her now.

"Aloha, Meg," Kahuna also added.

"Aloha to you two as well. Is this the pig you are cooking?" She admired the ground.

"Yes of course, this is a kalua pig being cooked in an underground oven we call an *imu*," Silas said.

"Interesting," Meg said, pursing her lips.

"You look beautiful this evening, Meg," observed Silas.

She blushed a little. "Oh, it's just the weather here. Nothing really."

"Oh, don't be so shy my dear. Everyone in Hawaii has this weather, but you look stunning." She blushed. He held out his hand to hers and she took it. "Come with me, I want to introduce you to some of our friends." They walked over to a group of people all wearing white.

Eight Foot was standing in the circle, smiling but not saying much as usual. Around him was Tom from Buffalo, New York, a mid-thirties white guy with a crown of curly brown hair and horn-rimmed glasses. His job for the community was groundskeeper. He was accompanied by Nathan—the librarian —who hailed from Ohio: a quiet, introverted guy who always stood as still as stone and only moved his head when he spoke. He had a black bush of hair and was the palest one there because he was usually ducked away in his room reading. And then there was the smart Hawaiian couple—Bane, a tall, fit, attractive man in his late twenties with a square jaw and hairless skin, and Lono, his charming Hawaiian wife who had big, beautiful round eyes and was carrying a baby in a front wrap over her stomach. Harvesting the various fruits and vegetables that grew naturally on the property was their main responsibility. Silas introduced Meg to each one, and they all greeted her with a friendliness she had seldom known back on the mainland.

"So where are you from, Meg?" Tom asked.

"Rhode Island, well now I live in East Hampton in New York."

"Really? You don't say. I used to live in New York State also, up in Buffalo, but the cold weather wasn't for me. I was freezing my ass off half the year up there. Glad I am here now where I can eat my share of papayas and mangos all day. What do you do?" Tom asked.

Meg was shy to say, so Silas swiftly answered for her, "Meg is the architect for the new compound we want to build on the Vortex. And my goodness, she is such a natural. You guys should see her drawings."

"I wouldn't go that far," Meg said, blushing with her arms folded.

"Oh, stop being so shy," said Silas, and pinched her arm.

"Oh, I can't wait to see what it's going to look like!" Lono said.

"Me too," answered Bane.

Nathan just nodded his head and agreed, "Yeah."

"Well, I am not done yet. You know what they say—design with the door closed, or else the creativity just runs away."

"I know what you mean," Lono said. "When I write, it's the same way. The moment I show someone half a story, I never want to see it again."

"Yes, I agree. The creative process is like that. You girls are so right," Silas said. "Anyone want to go eat some of our delicious kalua pig? I think it's almost done. I hear Biscuit over there barking at the ground for the good stuff." The group unanimously answered in the affirmative and they all began moving towards the *imu*.

In a minute, Kahuna removed the banana leaves and, with Eight Foot, lifted the cooked pig out of the earthen oven and over to a long wooden picnic table cut from trees on the property. Biscuit trailed them, barking wildly. Silas pointed a finger at him and he instantly stopped barking, sitting down in cooperation. Kahuna began pulling the luscious meat from the pig onto a big serving platter.

Along the same table, the Vortex head chef Beauregard Borderlon—a walking, talking real-life alligator from New Orleans, Louisiana—had prepared dishes full of love and happiness that he had the human sous chefs bring out. Yes, an alligator. For there are such things in the world as walking and talking animals and reptiles, and the Vortex had many such creatures. However, it was too early in Meg's awareness for her to meet them, and her mind was not ready for what was to come.

Although Beauregard was as Cajun as they came, he could cook any cuisine imaginable due to having listened to *The Food*

Network for years while being held in a pen at an old rickshaw two-pump gas station on the bayou. His cage master used to sit and watch reruns of Emeril Lagasse all day. Little did he know, Beauregard was quietly studying cuisine.

One day he escaped to Florida, where he was trapped by an old white man named Archie, who was running an alligator farm. At the time, Silas was trying to follow Meg's trace after seeing her in a vision near Miami while touching the stone. He stumbled upon Beauregard instead, communicated with him, and "pretended" to buy him in order to free him and take him to the Vortex where the mana of the stone would allow him to walk and talk, and fulfill his dream of being a chef.

Tonight, Chef Beauregard had prepared *poi*, a thick paste baked and pounded from the underground stem of the taro plant, loi loi salmon (Meg's favorite), hand-carved wooden bowls filled with white rice, bananas, *lilikoi* (passionfruit), pineapple, tuna poke (marinated sashimi tuna) and sweet Maui onions. Amazed by the feast, Meg filled her plate with all she could handle and sat down at a nearby table to eat. Silas sat down across from her while she ate, tossing food to Biscuit who was still sitting quietly.

Meg started with the pork, which was so tender; she savored the fatty, smoky flavor with long, slow bites.

"Good heavens, this is really amazing Silas, how often do you eat this?"

"Whenever we want." He smiled and paused, watching her. "Hey Meg, how are you feeling here now?"

"Good, I guess. I mean, I am a little worried about my family and job back home. I don't know, right now, I just love this food."

"I'm glad you are so present in what you're doing. Being in the here and now is all that exists," he said, and spooned some *poi* into his mouth, savoring it.

After the group ate, the night *mauka* rain moved in and the assembly dispersed back to their various bungalows along the property. The human sous chefs, Mickey and Banjo, cleared the tables quickly. Meg and Silas wandered over to Lono and Bane's white wooden bungalow, which sat to the east of the main house and to the south of the Field of a Thousand Hopes. It was lined in a row of other similar little houses where much of the community lived. The four sat on the porch and talked with the Hawaiian rain falling around them, massaging the tin roof.

"I love these neat little bungalows," Meg commented.

"They were a gift from my father to his workers, so they didn't have to worry about housing and could enjoy the land here with him," Silas said.

"Where did they all go?" Meg asked.

"When I inherited the land and house, I let them stay here of course, but a fire devastated the property and it was too much for them."

"We just love it," said Bane. "It's small, but just enough space for us and our daughter. I think if we have two children, we will need a bigger house though, Silas."

"Don't worry about it. Meg's building will have enough rooms for everyone. Isn't that right?" he asked her.

"Yes, I am afraid so," she said and laughed.

"Have you designed it yet? Tell us about it," Lono asked.

"Well, I don't want to give too much away for the time being but it's an extraordinary compound of stone buildings with domes and towers that scale down the mountain. It's more of a fantasy building than anything I have ever actually designed for a client."

"Gosh, I can't wait to live there, Silas. Hook us up," Bane said.

"You'll get the biggest room, Bane," Silas answered.

"Where is Biscuit going to live?" Lono asked. "He needs some proper digs."

"Biscuit's dog world will have a whole building with a view of the ocean, equipped with a king-sized bed and an endless supply of ribs—plus the occasional belly rub by yours truly," Silas said, and the group laughed.

After a while, Silas and Meg said goodbye to Lono and Bane, and then to each other.

As Meg ran back through the rain to the Tower, something in her heart emerged. A wave of emotion that she had never felt before—or at least not since she and Mick had first gotten married. She wanted to cry.

She didn't know why, but she missed Silas dearly.

"Dammit," she said, slamming the door of the Tower behind her.

17

M eanwhile, over in Hanalei Bay at Andy's Pawn and Gold store, Bernie slaved on the dual timer combination lock of the foot-thick vault door, sweat beading on his forehead when Red said, "We don't have time for this shit Bern, let's blow it."

Red grabbed the green military-issue rocket launcher he had purchased illegally on the black market in Honolulu out of the black nylon duffle, a full body shield and three black gas masks with noxious gas filters. He threw one of the masks to Bern and the other to Meathead and ordered them to put them on. Then he strutted over to the far wall while Bernie and Meathead donned the masks and took cover behind a upturned stainless-steel worktable, then he fired a single rocket at the vault door. It exploded in a fiery instant.

The store alarm blared overhead at a deafening decibel. After the gnarly smoke and dust settled, the three men walked inside the gold store's vault, where row upon row of gold ounces were housed, stacked on top of each other neatly on shelves: six hundred ounces of brick bullion to be exact—just over a million dollars' worth.

Meathead, a musclebound Polish guy with a bald head, grabbed the dolly and moved it over the rubble into the vault, where the crew began feverishly loading the bullion onto it. The gold was then trucked out of the service entrance.

Red had gotten copies of the exterior door keys and alarm code from a disgruntled employee named Ronald who got caught sleeping with Andy's seventeen-year-old daughter, Moonshadow, by another staff member. When Andy found out a few days later, he wanted to fire Ronald on the spot, but at Moonshadow's request, he gave him another chance. Hearing about the incident from a customer the other day at his jewelry store, Red approached Ronald with a proposition to be part of a heist. With revenge hot on his mind, he made copies of the store's keys that day. Three days later, he was fired when Andy finally couldn't stand seeing his face anymore.

After the six hundred ounces were boxed and loaded into the team's white van, the crew's driver, Mugshot, who was bald and never without a gold toothpick, sped away.

BACK AT THEIR hideaway at Hanalei Bay, not far from the famous surfer spot, the four were counting their gold in their underground bunker, a concrete-enforced storage room they had built below the A-framed beachfront bungalow—the perfect decoy.

"Looks like we won't have to steal again anytime soon boys. Wahoo!" Mugshot hollered and took a swig off a cold Heineken beer as he stood there in black lace-up military-grade boots, admiring all the seized gold.

"Yeah, well that may be true, but I am in it for the fame, not just the bricks," Bernie said.

"You can keep the fame, I just want the gold, that's all," Mugshot growled.

The four locked up the safe and went upstairs.

———————

DAWN WAS BREAKING, and just outside their back door, the waves were breaking too.

All four were raucous surfers. They donned board shorts and grabbed their sticks before running out to the water, the perfect ending to an all-night heist.

Some newbie was out and interfered with the lineup, so Red elbowed him in the eye, sending him running back to shore. All he saw was Red's right forearm tattoo of Poseidon before his face clashed with the water.

"Red, would you leave the kid alone? Seriously. Way to draw attention to us, you know! It's not like we just robbed a gold store or anything!"

"Aw, shut it mate," Red said with a thick Aussie accent. "Kid needs to take that shit back to the mainland where it belongs."

18

W hen Andy showed up at his store the next morning following a call from Detective Rogers, police tape was already wrapped all around the front of the barred store. Rogers walked over the crumbled debris on the vault floor. Seeing rows of empty red metal shelving, he asked Andy, "What were you keeping in here, buddy?"

Before Andy could answer, a calm man wearing a brown suit addressed Rogers, "You are on a need-to-know basis, sir."

"Says who?"

"Says me."

"Look, I am the lead detective here and I have a right to know what is going on!" Rogers commanded.

"The powers that be say you don't. I am with the Feds, and this is our jurisdiction." He put a hand on Rogers' shoulder as the two walked out of the vault. "Why don't you just go back downtown and have a nice cup of that garbage coffee that tastes like ant piss and one of those bad gas-station donuts and you'll be briefed later, *capisce*?"

Outside of the vault now, Rogers threw the agent's hand

away and yelled, stabbing a finger at his face, "I want to know what in the hell is going on down here!"

"Just go," the agent said. Noticing a bit of dried clear gel along the wall, Rogers didn't respond, and kneeled down to rake his finger across it. The agent, whose name was Mitch, kneeled too.

"What do you think it is?"

"I am not telling you, bud," Rogers replied.

"You really have an eye to spot that. Hey Bob, come see this. Officer Donut here spotted something along the wall."

Bob, a black man wearing a beige suit, came over and leaned down on his knees, "What is it?" he asked.

"Looks like Sex Wax to me. I wouldn't be surprised if it's a bunch of dudes here," Rogers said.

"Sex Wax? I don't copy," Bob said.

"S-u-r-f-i-n-g wax, you idiots. Geez."

"Oh, I see, are we through here?" asked Mitch.

Rising, Rogers pointed a finger in Mitch's face, "You're gonna hear from my chief about your treatment of me."

"Yeah, yeah, yeah."

ROGERS HURRIED off to call Chief Riley.

Riley answered, "Hey Rogers. What's new?"

"Chief, look, we got a situation down here at the gold store. Bunch of suit and ties are trying to shut me out. That's never happened before."

"Yeah okay, so what? I know the Feds are there. But there's nothing I can do about them not helping you out. I can't be there today. I'm sick with a brutal sinus infection."

"Well, it just pisses me off. I am not getting the respect I deserve here."

"Yeah, but it's out of our hands now, bud."

19

"Follow me," Silas said, ushering Meg through the waterfall from a path that ran alongside it, the mountain water cascading from a towering cliff of green vegetation high above.

Meg walked on through the waterfall, getting wet, her eyes aglow with wonder. They came to a broad steel door where Silas typed in a code; it slid open. Past the door was a dark cave —a lantern hung on the wall in the distance, where a native Hawaiian man was kneeling with a pickaxe.

Silas halted Meg and typed another code into a keypad on the wall for the alarm system; it beeped. Silas was wet as well, dressed in khaki garb with a desert army-fatigue canvas backpack, a panama estancia hat and a machete. He donned a headlamp, turned it on and continued on into the dark cave, ushering Meg to follow. They reached Kini, who traced his roots back to the famous surfer, Duke Kahanmoku, and had lived at the Vortex for a few years now, after hearing about it from some surfers around the island.

Meg asked, "What is this place?"

"This is our rock," Silas said, his voice ringing in echo off the walls. He paused. "It's where we mine our gold."

"Really?" She paused. "That's amazing."

Just past them, the rock stretched for as far as the eye could see. Kini set his pickaxe down and greeted them.

"Hi, I am Kini." He tipped his hat back and wiped his brow with a red-and-black bandana from his pocket.

"I'm Meg, nice to meet you. What are you doing down here?"

"Mining the rock," Kini said. "Why don't you guys stay here and watch for a minute?" "Okay, sounds fun!" Meg replied. They kneeled.

Silas pushed his hat back a little, his forehead dotted with sweat. "This wall is so amazing; it just drools money. And you know, money has to come from somewhere." He laughed a little as they watched Kini axe the wall, rock falling to the ground.

"I don't need any more money. I have enough of that. All I want is a kiss," Meg whispered, so Kini wouldn't hear.

Silas let out a chuckle, "Well, I would like to give you one right now."

Meg blushed and smiled. Silas touched her face with his left hand and the two kissed. They kneeled in silence while Kini resumed his mining. In her heart, Meg felt giddy. After a while, the two left, and Kini continued to work.

20

On Thursday morning, Silas was walking alone in the garden when two apapane red-feathered little birds landed nearby on one of the stone benches. He sat down beside them. They began chirping in unison. He knew they were asking for insects to eat, so he pointed to an area of the ground near the fountain and said softly, "Over there my little bird friends, you will find the best worms." The birds flew off directly to that spot, landed on the ground and began pecking.

Silas watched until both birds had black beaks full of worms, then continued his walk. Hearing an ant having trouble with a rock, he moved the stone out of its way. Then, he noticed the eucalyptus trees craning a bit more to the side than usual, so he went over and pressed a hand against one the tree trunks —the sweet branches eliciting that heady aroma he so adored. Through his palm he could feel the pain of the tree, longing for more water and wind.

Although it had rained a few nights ago, it had been a dry September, and Silas knew it was time. So, he decided to get the hose and water them. After feeding them, he walked back into the main house and down the long hall to his room.

21

Meanwhile, at the Police Headquarters, Chief Riley and Detective Rogers were bumping heads again. "How is the FBI involved with this gold heist at the jewelry store?"

Riley smiled. "They're in everything these days. Stranger things have happened."

"Yeah, but they keep butting me out. I want answers."

"Go down there and talk with them again. See if you can squeeze blood out of a turnip, but don't make me try. No sir, I am just here for the view. I transferred from a shit-detail in Seattle twenty years ago and never looked back, and I am not going to now. No sir."

"I will, you watch me," Rogers said, pacing the room. "Guy called me Officer Donut! Can you believe that? The nerve." He picked up the newspaper on the desk and held the front page up in Riley's face, "And now this!" He slapped the page with his hand. "Front page of *The Star Advertiser*... Officer Donut Misses the Mark. Fucking unbelievable!"

22

T wo days of work later, during which Meg was busy designing in her room, Kini had collected enough gold to fill his backpack and had just given it to Silas. Silas then paged Mickey through a loudspeaker system that was mounted throughout the Vortex.

Ten minutes later, Mickey wandered into Silas' office barefoot. The blond surfer had on a white tank top with matching board shorts.

"What do you need?"

Silas picked the backpack up off the floor and clunked it on his desk in front of him.

"We need to cash in some more gold, so we can buy supplies. Take it into town like you always do and sell it to Andy at the gold store."

"Sure, boss." Mickey looked into the bag. "Got a lot today, rad." He did the "hang ten" hand sign to Silas, who did it back as usual, laughing.

IN TOWN, as Mickey approached Andy's Gold & Pawn Shop in his beat-up white Toyota four-door Tacoma, he saw the police tape wrapped around the front and police cars parked all over the lot. It was the first time Andy's wasn't available since Mickey had been selling the community's gold and he didn't quite know what to do. He called Silas, who answered.

Mickey informed him that something suspicious had happened at Andy's. Although Silas felt it would be wiser to wait, he decided to ask Mickey to carefully locate another gold store this one time. He needed to buy supplies, and didn't want to access any of the gold in his hidden vaults. Mickey thought for a moment, then decided to drive a little further up the road to see if he could locate another buyer. A few miles away, he parked at Island Jewelry and walked in carrying the canvas duffle slung over his muscular right shoulder.

Larry, who had a pot beer belly and a large gold necklace, welcomed him in. Mickey talked with him for a moment, fishing about whether or not he bought gold.

"Sure, show me what you got kid."

"Okay, but I'd rather us do it in private, you know."

"Alright, alright...Tua!" Larry yelled to the other store clerk, a short Hawaiian with a grizzly smile.

"Yeah boss," Tua said.

"Watch over the store please."

"Sure thing."

"Right this way," Larry said, ushering Mickey to the back of the store, which had no windows.

Mickey set the backpack down on the worktable in the center of the room and opened it to remove a large chunk of gold rock the size of a baseball.

"What will you give me for this unrefined gold rock per ounce?"

"Shit mate." Larry picked up the rock and studied it. "Where did you get it?"

"Can't say."

Larry studied him, then looked back at it. "I will give you half the spot price of bullion if it passes the acid test."

"Give me seventy-five percent."

"Deal. How much you got?"

"Six hundred ounces, give or take a little." Mickey showed Larry the opened backpack; he glanced in.

"Sheesh mate, that's a hella lot. Don't see that much around here."

"I know, I know, look, do you want to buy it or not?"

"Yeah, yeah, hold your horses."

Larry slipped on his readers from around his neck and took the nugget over to his desk where he began to perform the acid test. Within fourteen seconds, the pair had their answer. Of course, Mickey already knew it was gold, but Larry couldn't believe it. Six hundred ounces of rough nugget from this silly surfer dude. Larry requested all the gold to be brought over to a large scale, so they could weigh it. Sure enough, it measured approximately 17 kilograms, roughly 37 and a half pounds.

"Seventeen kilos to be exact. Wait a minute," Larry said to Mickey. He went to his safe in the other room, where he unloaded 750,000 US dollars in rubber-banded cash—rounded down—while Mickey removed the gold and placed it onto the desk.

Larry set the cash down on the desk. "There you go mate. Count it if you like."

Mickey took his time counting it, and when he was through, he piled it into the backpack, thanked Larry and left.

BACK AT RED'S A-FRAME, Bernie received a call from his brother Larry in Kauai about the strange day's events with Mickey and the golden nuggets at their jewelry store. Bernie and Red had opened the store years ago, as a way to case potential clients on the island who they might want to rob, and as a means to fence stolen items to shady buyers.

"Are you serious mate?" Bernie asked, almost dropping the phone.

"Yes, I am not joking. This loser surfer guy is rich or something."

"Let's take a look." Bernie smacked his Bazooka gum.

"Okay, what do you want me to do, start surveilling him next time he comes to town?"

"Sure, let's get on it."

"Hey bro, you sure you want to do this? I mean you guys just heisted Andy's up the road. Time to take a trip. Take off. Disappear for a while. The cops will be looking for thugs."

"Yeah, yeah, yeah, well, a million bucks ain't enough to live on. We still got work to do on this rock."

"Okay, I get it. Your call. I'll put Bug on it right away and monitor this little shithead's actions. Tua can throw him in a volcano if he gets in the way."

"Good, get it done."

23

On Sunday, Sam, Mal and Peg met at the office even though they had the day off, because Sam was hysterical. He was wearing a super-tight navy-blue workout shirt and pink Lycra leggings with a matching pink baseball cap. He had grown a black handlebar moustache over the last week since Meg had gone missing because it made him feel heroic. When he wasn't at work pacing the floors, he was at the gym—working out was the only thing that had kept him from going insane.

Peg couldn't believe the whole fiasco either. The pair invented all sorts of strange scenarios for Meg. Sam thought maybe aliens had abducted her and taken her to the planet of Voltron to be her slave. Peg had bigger dreams for Meg, imagining that she had left to join a circus or something crazy like that. Now, even Mal was starting to get really worried. They had to answer Dawn and Meg's mother every day about whether or not they had heard from her. Waiting for Meg's next call had become the pair's sole obsession. Dawn had even quit her job temporarily in Brooklyn to move into her old childhood bedroom at her parents' house.

Today, Officer Henry called to check in with the office to see if there had been any sign of their boss.

"No, no sign, officer. We simply don't understand it. This is so not Meg," Peg said.

"Well, her sister Dawn and mother, Scarlett, haven't heard from her, either. And she isn't returning my calls. I'll check back in a few days and let you know what I find."

"Oh, thank you so much, officer." Peg hung up.

"Anything?" Sam asked.

"No baby, nothing."

"Aww shucks. Well, we will just have to keep waiting. What did the hunk say?"

"He said Meg hasn't return his calls either." Peg looked forlorn.

"Well, I won't stop until we find our dear Meg, dead or alive!" Sam boasted.

AFTER WORK, Meg's best friend—interior designer Sally Wooly—and Mal were sitting dockside at Louie's bar in Newport, after Sally insisted someone fill her in on Meg's whereabouts.

Sally had her beautiful golden-red hair pulled back into a ponytail, wore expensive jewelry and a black wooly jacket. It struck Mal as unusual because Sally's name was wool—guess she likes the fabric because of her name, Mal thought.

The unlikely couple had ordered drinks to oil the social wheels between them and were each about a gin martini into a decent buzz. Mal was loosening up and starting to talk about her love for Meg.

"I just have all these feelings for her now that she is gone. I can't explain it. It's like we have this connection." Mal looked dreamy.

"I know what you mean, she's my best friend. So, tell me what happened? Have you talked to her?" She stirred her martini with the olive crystal stirrer.

"No, no one has. That's the thing. She just left us with this one call to her mother that she was going to be working in Hawaii on this crazy project for three months. And now the whole office is on Bob's command. I mean we could go down like the *Titanic* if he can't pull this thing off. I am serious. It's scary."

"So strange." Sally breathed in deeply in disbelief and exhaled her worry. "Did she say anything about this note she found?"

"Note?" Mal turned to Sally and put a hand over her mouth. "No, nothing. What note? Tell me."

"Well, she texted me a few days ago that she found some bizarre note in a book and it had longitude and latitude coordinates on it for Hawaii. She did say she might go to see what the note was all about. You should check it out. I'll give it to this cop of yours. What's his name? Henry something?"

"Yeah, that's his name, Henry. My goodness Sally. That's it. That's what this is all about! I have got to go tell everyone." Mal jumped up, took a fifty from her wallet, slapped it down in front of Sally and put her black DKNY jacket on. "Sorry, I gotta go, girl. This is too important." Then she kissed Sally on the cheek.

"Okay, tell Officer what's-his-name to call me about the note. I'll fill him in."

"Okay, ciao girl."

"Ciao."

After leaving Louie's, Mal called Sam and Peg from her black Toyota Prius, informing them about Meg's note. Peg gave her Officer Henry's phone number, and she immediately called him after they hung up to relay the news about Sally and Meg's text and the note Meg found in the rare book addressed to her with longitude and latitude coordinates in it for Hawaii. He cleared his throat and told her he would reach out to Sally for the details first thing in the morning.

24

After sketching for some hours in the morning at the observation pavilion under the sun, Meg was being tormented by Biscuit, who had a three-inch hard turd sticking out of his butt where it was stuck, possibly from eating too many pig bones. Meg tried to dislodge it with her shoe, but it wouldn't budge. Then Eight Foot wandered over to ask her if she needed anything. Meg replied that she was fine, but what she really needed was some peace and quiet.

After Mickey returned from selling the gold, he entered Silas' office and dropped the bag of money on his desk. With hands on his hips, he explained how there was a crime scene at Andy's and he had to sell the gold to Island Jewelry instead.

"Hmmm, well, what were the police doing at Andy's?" Silas asked.

"I'm not sure, but the news will break soon on the tele, I expect."

Mickey, who worked as a sous chef and waiter at the Vortex's bistro for Chef Bojangles at night, had most days free, so he said goodbye to Silas with the intention to go surfing in the afternoon. While doing his manual sight surf report for the south coast at the observation deck, he found Meg and asked her if she would join him, but she wasn't interested. When he left, she was so distressed and unable to focus that she stormed off and locked herself in the Tower.

Huffing and puffing, she sat down at the drafting table in a frantic state; then she started drawing. Finally, for the first time that day, she could hear herself think.

She drew for hours and hours, not even stopping to shower. She hadn't missed bathing in twenty years, but she simply couldn't allow the flow of creativity to stop. Doing anything other than drawing broke her concentration. She drew for three days with no washing during the entire time.

Silas finally knocked with some food. As much as she wanted to see him, she had to call out to him, "Go away Silas, I am working."

She was now slaving away on the Theater building, giving it all her attention. This building's details and personality was telling her how to proceed with the next building—a kind of *piecemeal* growth concept that she had learned from a semester of studies with Christopher Alexander at the University of California, Berkeley. In fact, she religiously read *The Timeless Way of Building* by Alexander every year. From the reading, she knew that humans crave buildings that *nurture* them—buildings that had almost anthropomorphic qualities. She also learned not to take on any kind of ideology when designing, as she might fall into the trap of pushing her ideas on others who did not agree with her.

On the fourth day, she grabbed the ham and cheese sandwiches on gourmet rye Silas had left outside her door, and went to the Library on the second floor of the Tower where she started her real research into the kind of building she was seeing in her mind. Sitting in a cracked vintage leather chair by a circular window in the wood-paneled library, she ate her sandwich and read books.

Sifting through architecture books she had gathered from the various shelves, like *Early Medieval Architecture, The Story of Romanesque, Buildings of Hawaii,* and *Moorish Architecture in Andalusia,* she realized the building she had imagined was a combination of Romanesque, Moorish, Spanish and Hawaiian architecture. A strange mélange of styles, but she instinctively knew a way to go about it. Her creativity was now firing on all cylinders.

She still slept, but after five full days of work with not much more than a little food and coffee, she opened her door to see what Silas had left her to nibble on that morning. Still in her white terrycloth robe, her hair a complete mess, she looked like a zombie standing there. Sure enough, a plate of absolute tropical love awaited her—some Hawaiian poke: salmon on rice with a side of fresh mango and a coconut with the top cut off and a straw stuck in it. She brought the food in, ate it quickly, left the tray on her bed and proceeded to work for another whole day, running on sheer mania.

25

By Thursday, October 14ᵗʰ, the tenth day of no showers and sleeping in the same robe on top of the covers, Meg stank and couldn't see straight anymore. She had lost a good six pounds also. She decided to take a break long enough to brush her teeth and shower.

After drying her hair, she sat down at her drafting board and admired her frantic wave of work. The first three developed drawings were done, and they were very good.

At that moment, a knock sounded at the door. Meg opened it to Silas, dressed in board shorts and a white tank top. "Aloha Meg. How's it going? We haven't seen you in days, my dear. You look dreadful."

She laughed. "I just showered for the first time in a week."

"My God! That's too long for me, babe."

Meg thought Silas looked really good today, and did he just call her babe? She smiled, "Come in." She walked over to the drafting table. "Look at what I've been drawing." Meg rested her palms on her lower back. They looked at the drawings and she admired Silas' ruddy sun-touched skin as he stood there.

"Is this the Theater building?" (*Figure 10*)

"Yes, what do you think?"

"It's stunning! And this is the overall plan?" (*Figure 11*)

"Yes, the site plan...and I've developed the design of the entire palace further." (*Figure 12*)

"It's a masterpiece, brilliant! Your hard work has paid off. Why don't you take a break? We can go for a swim by the waterfall to celebrate, get your mind off all this work."

"Let me think." She was in a zone for sure, but Silas looked so good that she wanted to take a break now and go with him. "Okay, what the hell! This has been some very difficult work and I need to relax. Can Biscuit come?"

Silas laughed, "The old dog? Why of course. Put on your swimsuit and the trail shoes I left for you in the closet, and we shall go."

"Okay! Give me a minute."

In a few minutes, Meg came down to meet Silas. Biscuit trotted over to meet her as she exited the Tower.

"Hey Biscuit, sweet baby, how you doing today?" Meg said as he greeted her, smiling. She kneeled down to pet him and he wagged.

Then, Meg, Silas and the dog cut through the jungle down the long path to the waterfall, where the gold cave was located. She noticed that Biscuit seemed to move almost in unison with Silas as he followed his master. She had never seen a dog so attuned to another person. If Silas moved slightly to the right, Biscuit did too, and so on.

At the water's edge, Silas stripped down to his birthday suit. Grinning, he asked Meg to join him in the nude if she liked. Shy as she was, the thought of letting all that pretension go was exhilarating, so she hesitantly peeled off her bathing suit. Silas took her hand and they waded in.

The cool water touched their skin, and the Hawaiian sun broke through the canopy of green trees, tanning their cold bodies. Silas swam over to her, brushed her wet hair back and

Eskimo-kissed her—touching his nose to hers and wiggling it to the side a little.

Twinkling, she put her arms around his and a monkey called out in the trees. They started kissing. His attraction to her was as wild as the water bashing the pool.

When Biscuit jumped in, Silas laughed and swam over to the far side of the pool, where he ascended a steep trail that came to a rock outcropping.

At the top, he started counting in Hawaiian, *"Akai, ekua, ekolu."*

"No, don't!" Meg said. "It's too scary."

But he leapt off the cliff anyway, falling for what felt like an eternity to Meg. Splashing into the water, he burst up beaming. "Now you do it, girl."

"What? No way."

"Alright, be no fun." He treaded water, smiling.

"Okay, okay, sheesh. You gotta get your way all the time, don't cha?"

She swam over and made her way up the cliff nude. Biscuit followed her. After many false attempts by Meg, Silas instructed Biscuit with his mind to jump off the ledge in front of her into the pool below, belly flopping in the water. At that moment, *she remembered the dream she had about sitting on the ledge of the cliff looking down at the water below,* and she knew she had to jump. Falling far down into the cool water, she felt free —like life was a real joy again.

The whole experience of being at the Vortex was a drastic leap of faith anyway. It had been a year since Meg had let herself be loved, and it was taking time to open up again. Her life with Mick had been filled with his constant complaining: complaining about the weather, music at restaurants, the kind of trees in the Hamptons, her perfume. One time, he got irate on a beach trip to Maui and broke a plate in the kitchen of their rental house over the sound it made when it touched the kitchen counter. The nerve, she thought.

At first, she was furious at her sister for sleeping with him. Although the two girls hadn't spoken since Meg berated her on the phone the week after it happened, she had forgiven Dawn, her pride just hadn't allowed her to reveal this to her. In some ways, she had been grateful that her sister had given Meg a way out. It was on the rocks anyway—by the end of it, Meg was drinking a bottle of Merlot every night in the bathtub, wishing the whole thing would be over.

Silas was different than Mick. First, he was an artist, like her. His garden at the Vortex was a testament to his creativity. There was nothing between them to fight about. They had become best friends now. And Meg felt like that was the cornerstone of any good relationship—being good friends.

Silas and Meg dressed and returned to the main house where he followed her into the Tower with Biscuit hot on their heels. In the room, Silas threw her on the bed and she peeled off her shirt, throwing it out the open window.

"Oh no babe, my shirt just went out the window by accident," she said, and burst out laughing. Silas almost hit the floor laughing.

"Who cares?" he said, as Biscuit watched with disinterest.

Removing her shorts, Silas traced her body with the tip of his finger before the two made love to the sound of the birds in the trees, which flowed in through the open windows.

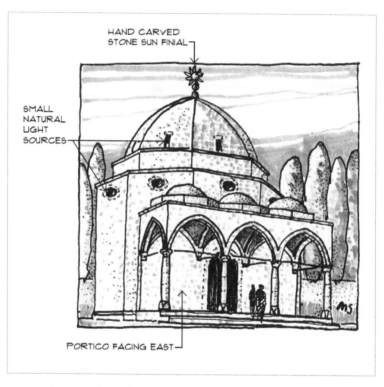

HAND CARVED
STONE SUN FINIAL

SMALL
NATURAL
LIGHT
SOURCES

PORTICO FACING EAST

Figure 10 *Theater sketch showing its hexagonal shape and its elegant dome all built out of the same stone.*

Figure 11 A more developed site plan.

Figure 12 *A more developed overall view of* Ha'alulu Maika'i *as it comes to life.*

26

Over the weekend, Meg directed her creative energies into the bed with her new boyfriend. She and Silas made love day and night.

Sometimes, they spent time in his bedroom also, which Meg observed had a very tall ceiling as well as artifacts from around the world on its walls and pedestals: carved African masks, Roman busts and stone moldings, etchings by Piranesi, Picasso paintings, framed Chinese robes, Indian pichwai paintings of elephants and parrots, exotic musical instruments, black-and-white photos of Silas with heads of state, shamans, and animals, of course, and all kinds of symbols and religious cosmology diagrams. The furniture was upholstered in exotic fabrics from Italy, Africa and India. Lanterns from Morocco, Italy and Spain adorned the wood-beamed ceiling.

And when they weren't in bed, she helped some in the garden. He taught her about the various island plants, and she would sit on one of the stone benches, watching him trim the topiaries, while drinking freshly made limeade. The Hawaiian rain moved in from time to time, washing the memory of Mick away from Meg, which had lingered on the dew of her mind for what seemed like an eternity.

Silas had used the $750,000 from the gold to buy supplies: $40,000 in food for the next few weeks; $310,000 to a local halfway house for battered women (which he ensured was always anonymous); $400,000 on supplies for the building project (paint, wood, nails, hammers, paintbrushes, plaster, caulk, buckets, etc.), plus $10,000 for a collection of Thomas Laird photographs of Tibetan monk murals signed by the Dalai Lama.

On Monday morning, Mickey and Kahuna went to pick up the food delivery in town at Island Food Suppliers with Silas' hauling truck.

There were hundreds of pounds of fresh seafood (whole fish and shrimp), grass-fed beef, spinach, chard, celery for juicing, leeks, plus three hundred potatoes, fifty ten-pound bags of white rice, boxes filled with mangos and papayas, eight big gallons of coconut oil, four fifty-pound bags filled with Kona green coffee beans and even more satchels filled with raisins, dates and macadamia nuts (Silas' favorite).

When he saw the shipment being unloaded at the walk-in storage fridge in the basement of the restaurant, Silas grinned a mouth full of whites.

Afterwards, he began a new topiary of two toucans.

In a bit, Meg walked over, "What are you creating today, honey?"

"A toucan for you. Wait, you'll see. It's going to be grand, like your vision for the house."

THAT NIGHT, after a delicious meal of loi loi salmon, Meg was restless.

The food had reminded her of the day she wanted the

salmon at the Saltbox in East Hampton. She didn't miss New York or her old job one iota, but she did miss the people, even Mal's bad attitude, and the reality of not being back in the Hamptons was settling in... and she couldn't help but worry.

What was she doing jumping off cliffs with a strange man in Hawaii who she had just met? Yes, she was in love with him now, but it was all so surreal and unusual. Her mother was probably crawling the walls by now and Meg couldn't stand the thought of it. She just couldn't do this anymore. It was crazy; any sane person would say so.

She tossed and turned all night. Even the soft twinkling island stars outside the windows didn't help soothe her mind. And the moment the sun came up, she woke Silas, complaining, "Silas, I must call the office."

"What for?"

"Because I'm afraid everyone is worried sick about me. What if Bob can't handle things without me and my business goes under? What then? I will lose everything if I can't make a call."

"Hmmm, okay love. But they're all asleep now. You can do it after lunch, but use my burner phone and only tell them you are in Hawaii. Do not reveal our specific location."

Meg agreed and Silas messaged Eight Foot to bring him the phone from his office downstairs. "I'm going to shower." When he finished, Silas slipped on a white robe. Eight Foot knocked with the phone and Silas answered, thanked him profusely and closed the door softly; then, he handed Meg the phone.

After lunch, Meg was squirming to call the office. She dialed.

"Hello, Summers & Company Architects, how can I help you?" Sam said in as chipper of a voice as he could muster.

"Hi, Sam, it's me, Meg!"

"Meg! Oh my goodness, you're alive! Where are you now?"

Sam put his hand over the phone to whisper to Peg that Meg was calling.

"I'm in Hawaii."

"Hawaii, girl, you go! Are you still working on that big project for the mystery client?"

"Oh yes, it is such a dream! And the weather here is to die for."

"Nice, you will have to tell me all about it when you get home. Hey, Sally told us all about the note. You know you don't have to lie to me? What's this all about?"

"The note. Aw, it's funny really. Well, I will tell you when I get home."

"Okay, when are you coming back?"

"I don't know. Soon...I'm not sure. Is everything okay at the office now with Bob running things?"

"Yes, I mean, I think so. Yeah, I guess so. Give him a call. I must say we've all been really worried about you. The police are even looking for you now."

"Okay, I'll call him. Just tell everyone I love them and that I'll be home soon to check on things."

"Okay, will do."

"Ciao."

"Bye, girl."

Silas joined her. "How did it go?"

"Good, I do feel a little better now."

"You know Meg, it's only to protect the Touchstone. Otherwise, I wouldn't care at all."

"I know, I know. I just worry."

"You worry too much, my dear. In the big scheme of things, what does it matter? People are born, they die, and are born again; people love, they hate, all the while, we are all just specks in the vast universe. The galaxies and the stars have been around for billions of years. Imagine that!"

"You're crazy," she said, smiling.

He Eskimo-kissed her again and said, "I may be crazy, but I love you."

"And I love you."

After that, Meg dialed Bob in Manhattan and they went over how he was handling everything with the office now that she was gone. He said everything was okay with the jobs, but that they had all been truly worried about her. He was relieved to know she was okay, and that everything would be fine for the duration of her absence. Thank God Meg thought to herself after hanging up.

SAM GOT off the phone and celebrated. "I think I'll wear my pink New Balances tonight and go dancing girl, just because Meg is alive. She's alive!"

"Tell me Sam, what on earth did she say?" Mal asked, intrigued by the call.

"She said she was in Hawaii."

"Hawaii, just like the note. Too much sun there for me," said Mal.

Peg clapped her hands and put on her lipstick. "I think that she just went off with Mr. Hunk Away and is in love. That's what I think."

"I want a Mr. Hunk Away Today," said Mal.

"Me too. I wonder if this Mr. Mysterious has a gay best friend for me," said Sam.

"You never know. He just might!" exclaimed Peg.

Sam called the police station to report the call to Officer Henry, who was relieved at hearing the news. Henry explained he hadn't made any progress determining who dropped the rare book or note at The Nook & Cranny for Meg, but with her calling in okay, there didn't seem to be much need to. He did ask Sam to keep him posted before they said goodbye.

27

It was Wednesday, October 20th. Bug knew the date because Halloween was approaching, and it was the only holiday he really cared for. From the window of his jet-black Cadillac, Bug—a too-pale-for-Hawaii high school dropout with a goatee and slicked-back curly black hair, dressed in a vintage flared-collared white button-up shirt and black polyester slacks—waited at Hanalei Bay, the Crown Jewel of the Northshore of Kauai, for the surfer that came into Island Jewelry the other day.

As fate would have it, Mickey showed up like he always did at five a.m., shortly after Bug arrived. He parked his Toyota Tacoma and hopped out, unstrapping his white board from the roof rack. He couldn't surf at the Vortex's cove because there were no waves there.

Bug rubbed his sleepy eyes, took a big sip off his coffee and looked at a still-frame photo of Mickey from the surveillance camera when Larry and he were doing the transaction, then squinted again into the distance at the golden boy. It was him alright, had to be.

Bug lit a cowboy-killer with his gold lighter engraved with a cow skull and blew the thick smoke, leaving the butt hanging from his lips. He could talk with it, walk with it and kill with it hanging there.

After what felt like an eternity, Mickey resurfaced, his blond curly hair wet and brushed back. A trail of girls followed him to his truck, where he continued to flirt with them while putting his stick on the roof.

Bug grinned, flicked his cigarette out the window and started the engine with his keys, a devil's cross-bone hanging from the keyring on a chain.

As Mickey slowly peeled away from the girls, Bug shifted into gear and tailed him. A few miles up the road, Mickey stopped by Sunshine Market for some cosmetic supplies and munchie food for the community that Silas never ordered: peppermint toothpaste, Oaxacan dark chocolate, shampoos and other essentials. Bug parked close by. Within thirty minutes, Mickey was carrying a cardboard box full of goodies out, which he proceeded to place in the Toyota's truck bed.

Mickey reversed and whipped out of the parking lot. Oblivious to Bug on his trail, high on girls and fresh waves, Mickey donned his shades and followed the two-lane road through green Hawaiian pastures where cows foraged on the richest grass on earth, grown in the mineral-soaked lava soil. After a few miles, he saw a double rainbow up ahead and when he reached it, he began to drive through it. The rainbow of colors kept appearing through his windows and he threw out the shaka "hang ten" hand symbol and howled through the opened window, "Wahoo! This is so rad!"

Passing through the double rainbow had about as much effect on Bug as breaking a chicken wishbone for good luck.

The two drove on up the lush mountain, curving around it until Mickey came to the entrance of the Vortex. He turned right into the driveway, opening the automatic gate with his clicker, and headed down the crushed-shell drive.

Bug parked up the hill away from the entrance. He always parked past his surveillance location—never before it—that way he wouldn't be noticed. There he waited, smoking Marlboro Reds.

After half an hour, Bug was through sitting. He got out and walked up and down the perimeter fence, which was a tall chain link with swirling razor wire at the top.

Not knowing what to do, he pinned the location on his cellphone and headed out. Dialing Larry back at Island Jewelry, he said, "I got 'em. Up Magic Mountain near the clouds. They got this big compound. And Larry...the fence is something fierce."

28

Sitting back out by the observation deck on another sun-soaked day, this one much quieter, Meg gazed out over the wondrous explosion of rock and vegetation and penned a poem about her new lover's enchantment with the garden.

When she finished, she walked over to find Silas trimming the hedges. He smiled and asked, "Why have you come, Meg?"

"Hey babe, I came to give you this. It's a poem. I wrote it for you." She handed him the folded paper.

Smiling, he took it and opened it. "How nice." He looked at her gratefully.

"You don't have to read it now," Meg said shyly.

"Why not?"

"Well okay, go for it."

He read silently.

Man of the Woods

In a beautiful garden he grows
A flower turned towards the sun
His eyes the color of chocolate cosmos
His lips the shade of a desert rose
His skin the color of honey
And if he cries Bulgarian rose oil falls down his nose
And there is sandalwood along his neckline
That smells like ancient civilizations
Where the essences of flowers were like gold
And his breath is lavender
Like Maui in the summer where horses still run wild
And he imprints the air with the scent of a thousand flowers
Of every shape and color
And his heart is a garden of roses
That will never wilt with the changing seasons
And in the center lies a perfectly formed one
He waters with his dreams
And the seeds of yesterday that
Never bloomed got blown away with the wind
Into the turquoise sea below
And when the rain falls from heaven he grows
With that spiritual nutrition that only the angels know.

SILAS CRIED A LITTLE, closed the letter, hugged her tightly, and said, "Thank you sweetheart. This is just what I needed." He paused. "Today we shall meet the builders."

"Oh really?"

"Yes!"

"Gosh, that's just what I needed."

Silas informed Meg the island stone masons were all very eager to meet their architect as the two made their way down to the site. He explained not only would they not be fazed by Meg being female, many were themselves female.

The first thought Meg had upon meeting them was that they were all iguanas. The whole crew. She was standing before what she could only size up as fifty thousand iguanas packed onto the large site.

"I know how shocked you must be, Meg. I did tell you I could communicate with animals already from my work with the Touchstone, and they can hear me and talk and walk from the energy here," Silas said calmly. "Now, let me explain further as I know how overwhelmed you must feel. These iguanas can lift the stone of ten men with their hands by working together, plus they do the job in half the time."

Meg started nervously shaking her hands at the side, and said, "What do you mean? *These are my builders?* What?!" she exclaimed.

"Honey, I thought you liked animals?" Silas said, winking at her, and walked over to pet the head mason whose name was Raphael.

"Yes, I do say, you are too frightened by us dear Meg," said the iguana, Raphael. "After all, we are only iguanas, not lions and tigers and bears—oh, my!"

Meg cracked a smile through her baffled gaze and spoke. "They are funny, too. Very good, Silas. Okay, so where do I start? How do I talk to you all? Silas, you're going to have to help me. I mean, this is really weird. These strange green lizards are my builders? I might be middle aged, but I'm not about to crack, am I?" She shook her hands some more, looking at Silas nervously.

Silas laughed, "Honey, you are home. These are our people, the earth, the wilderness, the iguanas." He walked over and placed his hands on the sides of her arms. "I promise you sweetie, *Ha'alula Maika'i* will be perfect. I swear. You'll see. Besides, this is the only way to do this, otherwise the Vortex would be crawling with people and someone might discover our Touchstone."

She hugged him. "I just don't want to crack, not this early in life. You know I could crack on you?"

"Hahahaha, who cares, we all go the way of the idiot some time or other. Let it be. Now, tell them hello."

"Hello everyone, I'm Meg. The architect."

"Hello Meg," they all said in unison.

"Okay, now let me introduce you to the rest of your team," Silas said. Meg relaxed a little after feeling the good vibes coming off her boyfriend in spite of the truly bizarre circumstances.

The two slowly walked to the other side of the property, where a line of animals sat to attention in a row. The first was a macaque monkey named Fuzzyhead, who described himself as a master timber framer with a crew of twenty-five fellow monkeys.

"Are you house-trained?" Meg asked.

"Haha, funny," Silas said.

"What about you? Do you go in the woods?" Fuzzyhead asked her.

"I guess so, if I have to."

Next down the line was Johnnie "O", the master plumber groundhog and his crew of fifteen; Samantha, a squirrel, who happened to also be the master electrician and her crew of seventeen; Halie, the orangutan master plasterer with her crew of twenty, and finally, Kadiff—the toucan master painter with a crew of fourteen.

"How do you do?" Kadiff said in a strong, elegant voice.

"Good, I guess. I mean, I'm here. I am a little funny about you being my painter, but I'm okay with it if you get the job done on time."

"Miss, I am Kadiff—I could paint this whole island like Picasso without flinching, what's it to you?" He scratched under his feathered wing with his beak.

"But you stink and you're not clean. You need to go bathe, all of you, before I have a heart attack."

The crew laughed.

"You're joking right? We stink to you, you stink to us. Get it?" Kadiff said.

"I get it, you're right. I was just joking. Now, let's have some fun and get started if you will."

Meg was out of breath—she was so busy processing it all. Just to think a group of animals would be working as her crew. It was unreal, however, her energy level and vision about the project quadrupled after she met the wonderful cast of characters, all assembled to build *her* masterpiece.

In the past, she had experienced so many problems with general contractors and their subcontractors that she had developed a severe case of post-traumatic stress disorder about it. She never knew when the next shoe was going to drop. Her anxiety levels concerning construction problems was the very reason she wanted to get out of the business almost every day back in New York. Now, she imagined that perhaps with magical animals doing the work maybe all her expectations about architecture and construction would finally be met in some inexplicable way, and she could be at peace.

She showed all the crew her many freehand design sketches that she had worked on so far. Their mouths and beaks dropped in disbelief at the beauty and grandeur of the palace. They explained they had been waiting their whole lives to work on such a masterpiece of imagination. Meg and Silas said goodbye to Meg's new team and Silas said,

"Now, let's go see your architects, darling!"

"Okay, sure! Wait, they aren't fish, are they?"

"Fish? No way!"

29

S ilas walked up the hill holding Meg's hand and when they got to the ATV, he asked, "Why don't you drive today. Think you can handle a four-wheeler?"

"Of course babe, I can do it all."

Silas got on and slid back, while Meg hopped on the driver's seat. Then, Silas showed her the controls from behind. It was romantic in a sweet way, with his arms coming around her from both sides, the warmth of his body pushing against hers.

Once she got the hang of it, she sped off into the wind with Silas hanging on gleefully from behind. He instructed her to head up the hill past the barn on the left. When they reached it, he told her to take a left a half-mile ahead. They were going to the old Congregation Hall, which Silas had ordered to be set up as a workspace for the architects.

When Silas and Meg walked up, Silas put his finger over his lips and opened the door softly.

The massive ancient hall was lined with drafting tables and work desks. Meg's mouth dropped, and when she noticed the room was full of black army ants, thousands of them, working together to move monitors and keyboards onto desks, she put a hand to her forehead.

"Come on girl, take it all in. These are our AutoCAD ants." Looking at Meg, who was now speechless, Silas moved in front of her and said, "Meg, I know it's a lot to take in, but they are excellent draftsmen. Seriously, do you really need a human to draw for us when we have these guys? Besides, they will cut the time down forty times or more. The whole thing might even be done in a week. Talk to them Meg. Tell them your vision. Let them know you are their friend."

Meg tried to speak, but no words came. Her eyes were still dazed as the ants scurried all over the floor. "Come on," he said, and walked forward. She followed, wide-eyed. In a while, her perplexity turned to amazement—sheer and utter bewilderment. "But how, how do you instruct them to do this? Are they dangerous?"

"Who even cares about it? I can *just do it*. Does it really matter? Just look at them doing their jobs. I wish *we could all work as efficiently as them*." The ants kept moving, while Silas and Meg walked down the long hall. When they reached the end, Silas said to her, "It's time Meg. Talk to them. Tell them about your dream, your project! They already have your preliminary design sketches."

She stood forward and the ants stopped moving, sensing her anticipation. Then, they turned towards her in unison. She was frightened but giddy at the same time.

"Hi, I'm Meg, your architect," she whispered so as to not deafen them, paused and swallowed hard. "I'm so happy to talk to you all today about my ideas in more detail, and especially in regard to the construction. The first thing we must do is have this entire building complex staked out on the site using my preliminary sketches. That way, we can all see what we are dealing with in terms of how the buildings will work with and interface with the mountainous terrain. As you may have already surmised, the buildings will, for the most part, appear to be rising out of the rough topography and not simply set on top of it. Let's go down to the building site so I can explain my ideas more clearly."

Silas carried ten of the architects, apparently the head of each production team, plus the queen, Camille, in a small golden locket with air holes on a chain around his neck, along with a small microphone with a speaker that projected the ant's voices. When they arrived at the site, Silas removed the ants gently and Meg spoke to them, "There will be four phases of general construction (*Figure 13*). The first phase will need to be the Theater, Library and Sacred Studies Buildings since these are at the back and at the steepest part of the mountain.

"The Library and Sacred Studies buildings will be cut into the mountain and the mountain will continue to slope down their sides to the first-floor levels, which reminds me, there will be five level changes as the various buildings descend the site.

"Phase 2 will be the first apartment building to be built, directly west of the Library and Sacred Studies buildings. It will start one level down. Also, part of Phase 2 will be Silas' house on the far end to the southwest. It starts on the lowest fifth level —after that, the mountain drops off too steeply, and will prevent any further construction past it. Another smaller apartment building will also be built at this time next to, and adjoining, Silas' house to the north."

"This sequence allows us to build Phase 3 in the remaining empty space. This phase will include two large apartment buildings, a coffee shop and a restaurant.

"The way that I have designed these buildings allows for beautiful courtyards and plazas to be built in all of the *negative* spaces between and around the solid forms. I have orchestrated the figure/ground between the buildings and the outdoor living spaces very carefully so that a complete Gestalt is achieved.

"Phase 4 is the construction and planting of these spaces.

This phase also includes an office/administrative building at the very front of the compound—the northeast end. The gravel construction drive will also be turned into a beautiful granite cobblestone street at this time.

"That's about it, do you guys have any questions?"

Camille, the queen ant, suddenly approached Meg and the worker ants carried the little microphone and a speaker in front of her. She rose up on her back two legs and spoke, "No questions yet our dearest Meg. We will start studying your design drawings and work on a schedule to outline our drawing time needed for each phase. Probably about three days for each phase. I'm sure I speak for all of us here today by saying how tremendously happy we are that we decided to answer Silas' call to join this remarkable endeavor. To be an important part of such an amazing project will fulfill many of our desires to create a new building with soul and *baraka*. We are all on our own journeys, and we feel like ours, yours, Silas' and everyone's here are merging in this time and space for a purpose."

"Thank you so very much, dear Camille," Meg said, touching her heart with her hand.

Meg was so delighted to hear this kind of response—she was not used to it from her fellow professionals. And now, here she was getting it from a group of ants. Amazing! "Wait, did she really just say only three days for each phase? I must have heard it wrong."

"No, you heard Miss Camille right. One to three days is all it takes these little wonder workers."

"My God!" Meg exclaimed. "That's otherworldly! It's out of this dimension. I mean, is that really even possible?"

"Yes, many things are possible when we use our minds in the right way."

"Okay, geez. I will have to get used to how different things are here. Silas, I'm tired from this meeting. All that energy from the ants wore me out. Can we go home, please?"

"Okay, but first I want to show you where our little ant friends live."

"Well, okay, only if it's not too far."

"No—it's just down the road." Silas and Meg picked up Camille and the other ants, placed them in the locket and drove them back to the Anthill where they said goodbye.

Then, Silas drove the ATV up the road right back toward the mountain into a small stone recess. They stopped and got off, and Meg soon spotted an amazing tiny ant city built along the base of the rocks that continued around the entire u-shaped recess of the mountain. The miniscule scale was hard to comprehend in that the "window" openings were just tiny dots on the surface of the sand metropolis. Ants were scurrying around everywhere coming and going in and out of holes and up and down ramps and streets. Meg thought it must be rush hour! There were lots of towers as well. High-rises? she wondered.

"What do you think?"

"Incredible! A far cry from the anthills back home. I've never even seen sandcastles that were this beautiful!"

Silas chuckled. "Well, they do have some pretty great architects living among them! In fact, they located this perfect spot which is protected from the north and west winds, as you've probably already noticed."

"I did indeed. It's marvelous, just marvelous. Thank you for sharing all of this with me dear Silas."

"My pleasure."

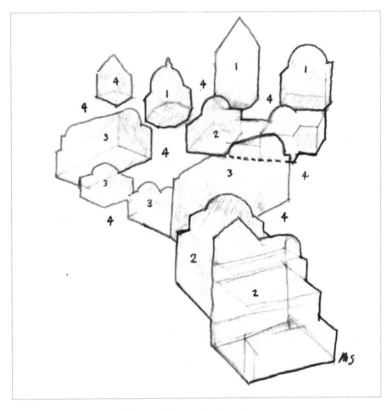

Figure 13 *Phases of construction 1-4*

30

That evening, there was a party in Meg's honor in the Garden. Silas had arranged for there to be all sorts of refreshments: wine, coconut water, pineapple coconut smoothies with rum and many other delicious treats. Bane had hand-turned coconut-cream ice cream made with real honey, and it was "to die for," as Meg said after the first bite.

Silas and Meg were talking with Bane, his wife and Kini about the day.

"So did you meet them, Meg?" Bane asked.

"Yes, I did."

"How was it?" he inquired.

"Yeah, did Raphael try to kiss you?" Kini joked.

"Not yet," Meg laughed. "It was...very...interesting, I might say."

Silas laughed a deep laugh and then sipped his piña colada. "It was a beautiful day full of wondrous moments with our fellow animal compatriots. She even went down to the Anthill."

Bane exploded with laughter. "The ants? Hey, did they bite you?"

"Bite me? No way. I'm their architect." She rubbed her arm freakishly.

"Hahaha, that's a bummer, they always bite me," Bane said. Meg's face turned sullen at the thought of her team attacking her with thousands of army ant bites.

"Not really dear Meg, they don't bite anyone. Bane is joking," Silas said.

"Hey Silas, why won't you let us watch any of the construction?" asked Bane.

"Well, I put that question to our animal friends, and they said because you stink."

Bane lifted up his arm, exposing his armpit through his white tank top, and sniffed. "Not me, I don't stink, ever. Come on Silas, let us watch for one day."

"Alright, alright, on the first full day of construction, October 29th, you may all join us. Bring a chair and some refreshments."

"Nice, thanks. You really are a gentleman Silas," Bane said.

"Hahaha, as are you! Alright, Meg and I need to go. Adiós. Stand proud, men," Silas said.

"We will." And Silas and all the men beat their chests like monkeys. Meg laughed.

"Boys will be boys," she said, amused. "Bye guys." She waved to them and they waved back.

Silas put his arm around Meg and they walked off alone through the luxuriant garden.

"Listen Meg, there is someone special I really want you to meet now. He isn't human and that shouldn't surprise you anymore."

"Oh no, should I be alarmed?"

"Hahahaha! Alarmed? Why, it's chef Beauregard Theodore Bojangles III from the bayou! He's an alligator."

"A *what*? Oh no, I am not doing this. I hate crocodiles."

"Hahaha, but he's the kindest old fellow man."

"Oh, he's a real person. Okay, good."

"Come this way."

Silas led Meg down into the Grand Kitchen of the bistro where Chef Beauregard Theodore Bojangles III was dressed in a starched white chef's hat and a clean white apron with his long gator bill sticking way out in front of him. He was at that precise moment holding a chef's stirring spoon full of some delicious-smelling Bordeaux sauce out to his long bill, his clawed, rough hand gripping it tightly.

When Meg saw him, she smiled. She wanted to be scared so bad, but she couldn't be. Not only was Beauregard not scary, he was hilarious standing in the kitchen like that, preparing a sauce.

"What you got there, chef?" Silas asked.

"Oh baby, I got a mean Bordeaux sauce to lay thick on some pork roast tomorrow night."

"Oh wow, can I try it Mr. Bojangles?" Meg asked.

"Alright sugarcakes, but make it fast and quick or I might eat you." He laughed. "I'm just joking babycakes; come on, get some while the getting is good."

She walked over and he scooped some up, feeding her the spoon. "That's delicious." She took it from him, scooped it in again and kept eating. "Oh my God, it's the best sauce I have ever tasted!"

"That's the spirit, hotcakes," he said, and turned on the stereo. James Brown's "Get On Up!" played, and the gator chef started dancing, his tail wagging back and forth.

"Aww shit, Chef Bojangles has done it now. He's gonna break it down for you bad chaps." He leaned forward, twerking his tail.

Silas clapped along and Bojangles started trying to dance with Meg, but it was no use. He was simply too big and his mouth got in the way.

"Good thing my wife has to be an alligator, or you'd be mine."

"Oh yeah big stuff, are you married now?" Meg asked.

"Hell naw, my ex-wife is down there in the swamp! Way down south. I ran away from her because she was bad, bad Leroy Brown on me. Put me in a pen at a gas station like I was some kind of circus animal. Naw, hell naw, not Mr. Bojangles. His crazy ass don't belong in no cage. That's when I busted out one night and made it to Florida where Silas and I met. And the rest is history. Now I am free."

Meg smiled. "Aww, she must be a tough lady."

"She ain't no princess, that's for sure."

"Hahahaha, it was so nice to meet you," Meg said. "When do I get to eat this French goodness?"

"Tomorrow night, and you can bet your bottom dollar there will be something sexy on the side just for you." He smiled, showing all his teeth.

"Alright Beauregard, I'll look for it."

"Don't tell Silas that you're my girlfriend now."

Silas laughed. "You're too funny for me Bojangles. Clean up this mess before the night ends or I'm gonna steal your key to the wine cellar."

"Hahahaha, alright boss, but you ain't getting that key ever. I stuck it where the sun don't shine. If you want it, you'll just have to come get it."

Silas and Meg laughed hysterically and left the wild chef alone.

31

"Silas, we are going to need an experienced general superintendent who can skillfully manage all of the craftsmen, and schedule them accurately. This is going to be a difficult and complex construction project as I'm sure you are aware," Meg said, then sipped her orange juice. The lovers were taking breakfast at the pavilion under a blue sky.

"Of course, my love, I have a very close friend. I guess you might say we are bosom buddies. He's been with me here from the beginning. His name is Carlos and he just so happens to be a master stone mason as well, and he is also highly intelligent, intuitive and will organize all the work. I know Raphael is a little hyperactive, but Carlos will keep him in line."

"Okay, that sounds promising, but where has he been all this time? I mean, why didn't you have him with me when I was meeting with all of the artisans? He would have had more gravitas and control over everyone."

"Well, this chap likes to keep to himself. He's a hermit really. I wanted you to be alone with the AutoCAD ants and some of the workers so that you could start to form a bond with them, and you've done a marvelous job. They all see your passion and your talent after your talks with them, and that is worth more than gold. Carlos has been here on the mountain all along, as this is his home. He has a wonderful old fort on the other end of the property that he renovated and added onto himself, with the help of other longtime residents. He's looking forward to meeting you today if that's okay with you."

"Sweet, babe! Of course, let's go see him!"

The two finished eating, and headed over to Carlos' fort by way of the ATV. When they arrived, Silas said, "Meg, I'd like to introduce you to my dear friend, Carlos."

Meg leaned a bit to the left, where she saw a giant orangutan climbing over the top wall of the fort, scaling down the stone wall towards them (*Figure 14*).

Carlos walked up and extended his big ape hand to Meg, who took it reluctantly.

"It's so nice to finally meet you, Carlos. I've heard so much about you. I was so glad to hear from Silas that you are an experienced builder and that you will be our superintendent."

Carlos—a swirl of energy, movement and verbalisms replied, "Hi, Miss Mag Pie!"

"No, it's just Meg."

"Okay, Megus Pegus."

"Let's talk business, shall we?"

"Will do Megaroni!" He showed a toothy grin.

Silas interjected, "Come on, Carlos—that's enough. I know you are excited to meet Meg, but she really wants to talk about the building."

Carlos straightened up, "Oh, all right. Meg, I have special abilities as you can see, since I can talk to humans, but I can also communicate with all animals the way Silas can. With this." And he pointed to his brain with his left pointer finger. "Silas and I grew up together here on the island. We are both so grateful to be able to do this because we learn so much from our brothers and sisters of the earth. They learn from us as well. Our animal friends are so much more talented and intelligent than humans know, especially when they have the powers of the Touchstone. So, over the years, we have taught them to perform certain construction tasks and now they are all extremely proficient and they take enormous pride in their work. You have met many of them already, but not all, since Silas didn't want to overwhelm you.

"Let me give you a run-down on the rest of them. There are monkeys who will build all of the domes and barrel vaults. Then the squirrels will install the lighting. The ninth group are the mice. They will install the air conditioning, which will be achieved by hot and cold water piped in all the floors. Okay, you can talk now, Megaroni."

"Interesting."

Carlos shifted his weight. "Why, Meg darling, it's as fast as lightning with our dear animal brethren doing all the work. You'll be amazed."

"I already am. How fast?"

"Well, I put the question to each of the craftsmen in the nine groups, and after much thought and debate, they came up with nine days each. That is eighty-one days total for each of the three phases instead of your four, so it is 108 days total." (*Figure 15*—which will show how the three phases overlap)

Meg put her hands on her hips, leaned forward a bit and said, "Well, that is the craziest and dumbest thing I've ever heard. Are you pulling my leg Carlos?"

Carols shrugged and turned his palms up, "Now, why would I want to do that?"

"First off, nine days is completely absurd. Why would each specialty, which are all different and which would clearly take less or more time than the others, all be the same nine days?"

"Well, it's not an absurd amount of time to them. In fact, they wonder why humans take so long! You know, animals are incredibly focused by nature. I asked each of them that same question and everyone said they like the number nine, and furthermore they like the number eighty-one for the total days of each phase, because it's nine times nine. They said it all has a nice symmetrical sound and feel to it."

Meg threw up her hands, "Well, that is even more absurd than before. I'm sorry I even asked the question!"

Silas jumped in, "Now, Meg, you will need to suspend your beliefs about all of this, but I'll tell you one thing: it will be the most fun you have ever had with your clothes on. You and I will go to the site each day to watch the activities. It will be the greatest show on earth, one you will not want to miss!"

"Oh, all right. But I'll have to see it to believe it. Carlos, thank you so much for meeting with me. Now I realize that you must be the key ingredient to this crazy party we're about to throw."

"No Meggie Honey Pie! Not me, but you! You are the star of the show." He bowed.

That night, Meg and the whole community planned to dine in the old fort café at seven pm. At six-thirty, Silas arranged a viewing party of his recently purchased Thomas Laird photographs of Tibetan Buddhist monks on display in the downstairs entry hall to the café. The Taschen *Collector's Edition* was truly a masterpiece, signed by his holiness, the 14th Dalai Lama. It sat on a Shigeru Ban bookstand, and each person donned gloves before looking through the exquisitely painted murals in the book.

After mingling for a while, the group gathered upstairs to dine on Chef Bojangles' scrumptious roasted pork with that delicious Bordeaux sauce Meg adored drizzled all over it. Accompanying it was a side of buttered white rice and green chard. Not only was the meal delicious, it gave Meg the sustenance she needed to fend off the fatigue from a long day of meetings in the hot sun. Meg's special extra side dish Chef

Bojangles promised her wasn't there, and she knew he had forgotten it, but he didn't appear, so she was unable to ask for it.

Figure 14 The fort house for Carlos and his large extended family

Construction Schedule:

Phase 1

Masons: Iguanas	1	2	3	4	5	6	7	8	9
Domes & Barrel Vaults: Macaque Monkeys	10	11	12	13	14	15	16	17	18
Timber framers: Rhesus Macaque Monkeys	19	20	21	22	23	24	25	26	27
Plumbers: Groundhogs	28	29	30	31	32	33	34	35	36
Electricians: Squirrels	37	38	39	40	41	42	43	44	45
Air conditioning: Mice	46	47	48	49	50	51	52	53	54
Plasterers: Orangutans	55	56	57	58	59	60	61	62	63
Cabinetry: Chimpanzees	64	65	66	67	68	69	70	71	72
Painters: Toucans	73	74	75	76	77	78	79	80	81

Phase 2

Masons: Iguanas	10	11	12	13	14	15	16	17	18
Domes & Barrel Vaults: Macaque Monkeys	19	20	21	22	23	24	25	26	27
Timber framers: Rhesus Macaque Monkeys	28	29	30	31	32	33	34	35	36
Plumbers: Groundhogs	37	38	39	40	41	42	43	44	45
Electricians: Squirrels	46	47	48	49	50	51	52	53	54
Air conditioning: Mice	55	56	57	58	59	60	61	62	63
Plasterers: Orangutans	64	65	66	67	68	69	70	71	72
Cabinetry: Chimpanzees	73	74	75	76	77	78	79	80	81
Painters: Toucans	82	83	84	85	86	87	88	89	90

Figure 15 List of artisan categories and their construction schedule

Phase 3

Masons: Iguanas	19	20	21	22	23	24	25	26	27
Domes & Barrel Vaults: Macaque Monkeys	28	29	30	31	32	33	34	35	36
Timber framers: Rhesus Macaque Monkeys	37	38	39	40	41	42	43	44	45
Plumbers: Groundhogs	46	47	48	49	50	51	52	53	54
Electricians: Squirrels	55	56	57	58	59	60	61	62	63
Air conditioning: Mice	64	65	66	67	68	69	70	71	72
Plasterers: Orangutans	73	74	75	76	77	78	79	80	81
Cabinetry: Chimpanzees	82	83	84	85	86	87	88	89	90
Painters: Toucans	91	92	93	94	95	96	97	98	99

Phase 4

All Paving & Planting: Silas and his crew	100	101	102	103	104	105	106	107	108

Figure 15 List of artisan categories and their construction schedule

32

On Friday, the 22nd of October, the weather was cool and surreal. Carlos and Meg met with the head of each of the nine groups of artisans (*Figure 16*) down at the building site to talk about the schedule for Phase I.

"Thanks for meeting us today," Carlos said, addressing the group. "I'm going to lay out the schedule, which is fairly simple and easy to follow.

"The iguanas will start placing the stone in a week immediately after the excavation for Phase I has occurred, and they will have exactly nine days to do so. They will be building the exterior shells and interior bearing walls for each of the buildings.

"The masons' macaque monkey crew will build all of the stone domes, barrel vaults and pitched roofs in nine days. In fact, the buildings in this phase have all the roof types that will appear in the finished compound.

"The rhesus monkey timber framers will have nine days to install all of the timber beams and flooring for each floor. The stone masons will allow a six-inch stone ledge around the entire interior perimeter of each building for load-bearing purposes. There will also be interior stone columns and walls for the timbers to bear on.

"Our plumber friends, the groundhogs, will have nine days to install the plumbing. Hi guys...you will burrow under the basement floor to install the in-ground pipes, but the rest of each building will be easier to get to since all the wood floors will be exposed...and there will be open chases in the stone walls for vertical pipes that will be filled in once you are finished. You will also install the site plumbing from each building. I'm sure you have studied those drawings and details from our civil engineer ants.

"Our squirrel friends will have nine days to install all of the electrical wiring which will run under the floors (by the way, in the basement, chases will have been installed under the timber flooring for you to use) and in the walls (chases will have been installed in the stone walls as well). Plugs will be in the floors only—not in any of the stone walls. Also, you will be installing all of the light fixtures, which I understand you already have on the property.

"And the mice will install the air-conditioning and heating. As you know, this will be handled in a piped-water system that will run under all the floors. You've already run the main lines from our energy source to each building site, so you should be good to go. Have fun!"

"Whoa! What energy source? No one has explained this to me!" Meg said.

"Hold on to your hat there, Meg-a-thon," Carlos said. "Aren't you glad you don't have to worry and think about that? Silas will fill you in on this...it's quite extraordinary."

"Okay, okay, it's just a lot to take in all at once."

Silas spoke, "Our orangutans will be our plasterers. They will also have nine days. Guys and gals, Meg will want to meet with you tomorrow to discuss the exact finish she's looking for."

"Good, Meggy Head. The chimpanzees will produce all of

the doors, windows and cabinets in their shop over by the ant barn," said Carlos.

"Hi, my monk-monk friends. How are you?" said Meg, addressing the monkeys.

"We're great and excited to be here," replied the head chimpanzee, Harry, showing his teeth. Then, he began picking his nose in a playful manner, while Meg watched in horror.

"I can tell, a little too excited with that finger of yours." Harry scratched the top of his head, acting confused, then showed his teeth again. Meg shook her head smiling.

"Anyway, all of the doors and windows will be made of teak and left unpainted. But the cabinetry and shelving will all be painted oak. The painters are our toucan friends. We welcome you. There won't be much for you to paint, but nonetheless it will be very important work. You will be painting the underside of the domes, barrel vaults and pitched roofs, which will have been plastered by the time you arrive on the site. And, as we've already discussed in private, this will be very exact and beautiful decorative painting which Meg is still designing and drawing. She will be finished in time for you to start and I think you will be pleased. You will also be painting the interior cabinets and shelving, but they will be simple colors, a 'no-brainer' for you Michelangelos!" said Silas.

"I'm so impressed by you all. You are such brilliant, talented, and well...just amazing people—uh—I mean animals. Please forgive me; I'm new to all of this," said Meg.

The animals cried in unison, "We forgive you Meg—you're not such a bad animal—uh, we mean—person."

THE ANIMAL ARTISANS

RAPHAEL
THE HEAD OF THE
IGUANA MASONS

FUZZYHEAD
THE HEAD OF THE
MACAQUE MONKEY
STONE ROOF MASONS

JUMPY
THE HEAD OF THE
RHESUS MACAQUE
TIMBER FRAMERS

JOHNNIE-O
THE HEAD OF THE
GROUNDHOG
PLUMBERS

Figure 16 Animal Artisans

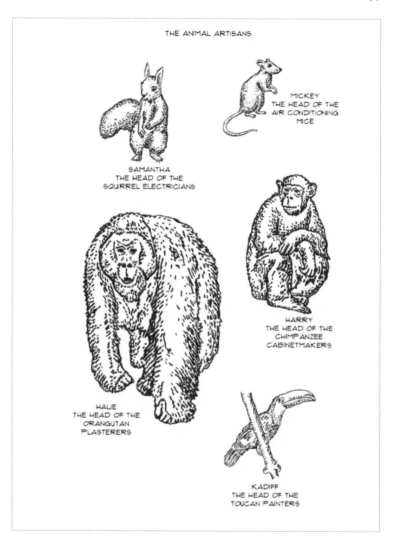

THE ANIMAL ARTISANS

SAMANTHA
THE HEAD OF THE
SQUIRREL ELECTRICIANS

MICKEY
THE HEAD OF THE
AIR CONDITIONING
MICE

HARRY
THE HEAD OF THE
CHIMPANZEE
CABINETMAKERS

HALIE
THE HEAD OF THE
ORANGUTAN
PLASTERERS

KADIFF
THE HEAD OF THE
TOUCAN PAINTERS

Figure 17 *Animal Artisans*

33

The next day, Meg arranged to meet with the plasterers. Addressing the assembly of orangutans with the leader Halie at the front, she said, "Hello everyone—I realize that the stone masons will have all the fun before you can actually start your work." The group laughed. "But, as soon as they get each building enclosed and after the timber framers, electricians and plumbers have finished, you will be able to start the interior plastering. For the most part, all of the interior walls will be smooth white plaster; however, there will be cases where we decide to allow the exterior stonework to be exposed. The AutoCAD ants will show most of these areas on the drawings, but I suspect that as I see the actual spaces and how the natural light hits certain stone walls during the day, I may improvise, which I am known to do, and after those drawings, of course, you'll be the first to know.

"The most important thing I wish to mention to you all today is that I am going to want to see a most sensitive application of plaster to these stone walls, so that the plaster does not end up perfectly flat. I want you, the plasterers, to get a feeling of the stone when you are plastering over it. I don't want to follow the stone surface literally, but rather for you to create a surface that is almost flat but isn't—it will have a life to it, like the skin of a living thing. The masons will have about thirty small stone walls for you to experiment on sometime next week. I will also want you to test different tones and shades of white: a soft antique white being the most desirable. Other 'whites' that aren't selected may be used in certain specific areas, so be sure to save all of the formulas."

Halie said, "I just downloaded everything you said to the computer in my head and it will be absolutely perfect, Miss Meg." Halie then bowed. "At your service."

"Thank you Halie!" And Meg bowed back. Then, Halie wandered off, making the kind of noises that monkeys make.

On Sunday, Carlos arranged for Meg's excavation meeting to be with the five main iguana stone masons: Raphael, Don, Tom, Bon and Fron. Silas hung back with the other iguanas to entertain them with fire tricks, at which he was truly an expert.

The iguanas needed to start site excavations for Phase 1 as soon as possible to get the project rolling. Raphael asked Meg to explain her vision to them. His little tongue flipping out freaked her out at first, but then she thought her tongue probably freaked him out, too.

"This group of buildings will be a living, breathing part of the site—of the mountain itself. You will have to excavate all the stone you need from the construction area itself. How you are going to do that, I have no idea."

Raphael lit a cigarette in his iguana fingers and started smoking.

"You're...you're smoking now?"

"I always smoke, it helps me relax. Silas doesn't like it, but what he doesn't know, won't hurt him, right tootsie? Tell me more, sweetheart."

"Okay, okay, I can do this. It's not any worse than an average Tuesday in New York." Composing herself, she continued. "The surveyor will stake out the entire area in a few days and the architects will have drawings for you that will map out every level of cut in feet and inches. But here's a quick sketch (*Figure 18*) for the first phase of excavation so you can get a rough idea of what we are doing."

Meg showed Raphael the sketch, which he studied with curious eyes.

"At the top of the sketch, you can see where the mountain is allowed to enter into the basements of the Library and the Sacred Studies Building (*Figure 19*), as well as into the courtyard between them. I like the mountain and the buildings communicating in this way whenever we can allow for that. Because we are going to start on this before we have complete precise working documents, these early drawings will give us deeper and wider measurements so we can fill in later if we need to. You will quarry and cut the stone on site and the excavation cavities will become basements for each building. Each building will rise out of its own site using its own materials— this is the timeless way of building. Also, I should note: when we get to the last building phase, you will then move your stone cutting operation to the north side of the site.

"I hope that all of you with your love of stone have been studying the native material in this area and at our building site."

"Of course, sexy legs," Raphael said.

She smiled, then took his cigarette out of his mouth, stepped on it and then picked it up and put it in her pocket. He grunted at the action.

"Well," Meg continued, "it's a beautiful stone with a nice surface quality. What I would like to see from you and your masons are sample walls showing us the many varying ways it can be laid, including more formal as well as more rustic methods. There will be different kinds of buildings within the walls of the compound that will require different types of stone masonry techniques: ashlar, rubble, chopped—some with tight joints and some with large mortar joints. Please study the historical models used on this island, even though we may or may not use those. However, if we all agree, we may use them here and there as needed. Also, as you've seen in my sketches, there will be stone barrel vaults and domes to be used as exterior roofs. Please prepare samples for those as well. Once we start on the first building, which will be the Theater, we will know exactly which stone-laying method to use."

"Are we through?" Raphael asked.

"Yes, you can go. Come on, get started."

"Look ma'am, we got this. I got this. I am Raphael, the king of the iguanas. We are here to build this beautiful vision of yours, Megaroni. We know that if the Touchstone has selected you as the architect that we are in the very capable hands of a true artist. We look forward to working hand in hand with you as we live and learn from each other."

Moved, Meg decided to lean in and give him a kiss on his check and wondered if, maybe, he would turn into a prince or something like one of those frogs in the fairytales she read when she was a child, but he didn't. Instead, he just smiled and said, "*Mi amore, sei bella! Ciao!*" And he left with his team, yelling back to her, "I will see you soon. Be there or be square! And remember, it's not hip to be square. I like Huey Lewis and all, but he's wrong about it."

Meg laughed, "Okay, I will be hip, not square. See you soon Raphael!" And she waved goodbye to him.

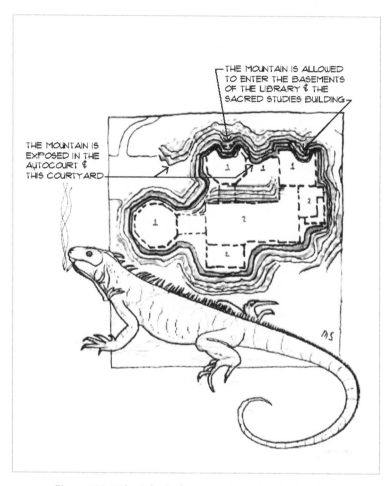

THE MOUNTAIN IS ALLOWED
TO ENTER THE BASEMENTS
OF THE LIBRARY & THE
SACRED STUDIES BUILDING

THE MOUNTAIN IS
EXPOSED IN THE
AUTOCOURT &
THIS COURTYARD

Figure 18 *Meg's sketch for the first excavation, and Raphael, the head iguana*

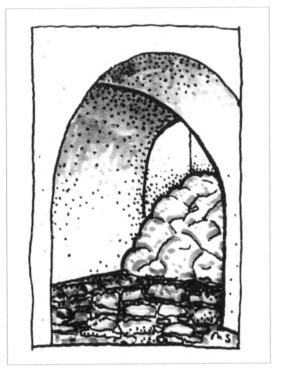

Figure 19 *Mountain coming into the Library basement*

34

T he crew of four misfits had been lying low since the heist at Andy's gold store. They had all moved their things away from their hideout on the beach to Bern's place in the hills, The Pirate's Booty. Secluded, it was on land surrounded by forest, so they could rest easy that no one would spot them there. Plus, there wasn't the constant temptation for the crew to catch a wave at Hanalei beach.

Today, they were all shirtless, exposing their various tattooed bodies. Restless and agitated after being indoors for so long, they all agreed to take a chance and go out for some pizza. So, they shirted up and packed into Red's Ford F150 black Raptor and headed to their favorite Italian joint down the hill, called Little Italy's.

The group ordered two deep dish pies with extra pepperoni from the owner Bob and drank iced beer from bottles, while playing the Pac Man game in the corner—their favorite pastime.

"Dude, I am so bored lying low like this. I can't take it anymore," Red said, popping his neck from left to right, while watching Meat and Mug play.

"You know what we should do, hire some strippers to come give us a bunch of lappies at The Booty," Mug said, taking a swig off his Heineken while controlling the joystick with his other hand, a single silver skull ring adorned the index finger of his fighting hand.

"Yeah, that's about the wackiest thing I have ever heard Mug," said Meat. "You know how it is with strippers, you can look, but you can't touch."

"No, you got it wrong Meat, it's look, but can't feel," said Mug. Bern and Red clanged beer bottles, and everyone but Meat laughed.

Red's face became serious as he addressed the group sternly. "Look boys, I see this surfer freak that came into Island the other day being our ticket out of here. I think this is gonna be the big one. The score of a lifetime. Make all our dreams come true. And I'm not talking about any old lap dances with some trucker girls from Jersey after this one. I am talking about trips to Spain in our jet. And millions and millions of dollars."

"I don't see it Red. What you smoking anyway? Some blond surfer loser answering all our dreams. Get out of town," said Meat.

Red fake-punched Meat, who flinched, then laughed.

"Dumbass. I got bigger dreams than you dipshits. We'll know soon," said Red, and he got up and left to go to the bathroom.

———

MEANWHILE IN RHODE ISLAND, it was 7 pm and Sally, Dawn, Mal, Sam and Scarlett were all dining together at the farm to table hit restaurant Brix connected to Newport Vineyards in Middletown.

They were currently sharing a baked brie appetizer and

three duck confit and fig pizzas, now on their third bottle of
Gemini Red. The place was bustling tonight, a clatter of wine
glasses and chat from the surrounding tables.

"So did you ever make it to The Testicle Festival, Sam?"
asked Peg.

"No, I missed the Florida one this year due to this whole
fiasco with our Meg."

"Hey, I want to go!" said Mal.

"What is it again?" asked Sally, looking puzzled.

"It's a bull ball festival down near Miami. I go every year.
And yes, Mal, you're invited now next time." The table laughed.
Sam took a sip of his wine, then winked at Mal.

"A bull ball festival?" Sally asked disgruntled. "What, do
you eat them?"

"Well, I don't, but a lot of people say they taste just fine,
especially when they are battered and fried." More laughter
erupted from the group, but Sally just shook her head in
complete disbelief.

"So, where are we guys? Any more news from our girl?"
asked Peg.

"No news," said Scarlett.

"Hey, no news is good news, right?" added Dawn.

"I hope so," her Mom said.

"I want to run off one day and disappear with Mr. Hunk
Away," said Peg.

"You and me both," added Sally.

"Do you really think she is with a guy?" Sam asked Peg.

"Well, I hope so. Hey, at least, its dreamy that way."

"Yeah, this client thing is too mysterious and strange. Three
months with no outside contact. Who does that?" asked Sally.

"Well, I hope she calls soon so I can sleep again at night,"
her mother remarked, then finished her wine."

"You and me both," added Dawn.

"Amen ladies, let us toast to Meg's homecoming," said Sam, raising his glass. And everyone lifted theirs as he continued, "To Meg," and they said, "To Meg," and he followed with, "May everyday bring her more happiness than yesterday."

35

W hen the fifty thousand iguanas arrived at the site to start excavating the stone for Phase I, Meg and Silas took a front row seat on the mountainside just above the area to be excavated.

At that moment, thousands of ants marched down the hill carrying a roll of plans. Carlos, Silas, Meg and Raphael all applauded gleefully. Then, the ants magically climbed a work-table Carlos had set up that consisted of a big slab of wood balanced on two large stones and rolled the site plan, excavation plan and detail sheets out on the table; then, they left just as swiftly as they had come.

Carlos and Raphael started studying the ants' drawings. Raphael had a cigarette hanging out of his mouth while he talked with Carlos. They conversed for a while, and then Raphael showed the drawings to the head of each team. The surveyors had already staked out the plan areas, so they simply needed to know the desired depths for the basements.

"Raphael, are you smoking again?" asked Silas.

"No," Raphael said, the cigarette still hanging in his mouth. "It just seems that way."

Silas chuckled, then Meg asked him where their equipment was, and he said, "Oh, they don't need any—they will use their teeth for cutting and their own bodies for lifting."

"Oh, Jesus! How's that even possible?" Meg responded.

"Well, they have very sharp teeth and in groups, they can lift very large stones," Silas explained.

"Oh, I see."

"Don't you get it honey? It's us! The Pyramids, The Sphinx, Stonehenge, Machu Picchu, they did it. They did it all."

"After meeting these little guys, I believe it!"

"Just watch. It'll be the greatest show on earth!"

Meg thought a minute then said, "Well, yes. Okay, but if I get overwhelmed and go a little crazy, promise me you will take me to the looney bin?"

Pulling her in for a firm hug, Silas said, "You got it. Looney bin or bust. Here we go." Before releasing her, he planted a firm kiss on her cheek.

In one exact moment, en masse, the iguanas started chomping at the stone, so quickly that Meg couldn't quite tell what was happening. But as she watched, somehow miraculously, a hole started to develop and large, carefully stacked piles of chopped stone started to appear next to it on the Phase 3 area of the site. They would use these to construct the Phase 1 buildings.

Watching in complete and total amazement, the hole grew larger and more defined, and the stacks grew larger and more organized as Carlos expertly directed the team.

Silas asked Meg if she wanted to take a break and get some lunch.

"Hell, no! I wouldn't want to miss even one second of the most thrilling show on earth. I love it!"

Silas smiled to himself and knew she was *hooked*.

At exactly six pm, the iguanas were finished—the work was perfect, Meg said. She thanked Raphael and his crew and congratulated them on a job well done. He blew smoke her way and apologized.

"You won't get my cigarette butt again my lady, but I will take another kiss if you have one."

Meg kissed him politely on the cheek and he beamed.

AT DUSK ON MONDAY, October 25th, Meg and Silas went to the old fort café for a bite to eat and raised their glasses of red wine, toasting the first successful day of the building process.

"I toast to you, my darling, for the design of our *Ha'alulu Maika'i* and to the first preliminary day of its construction."

"And I toast to us and the Vortex and all of our extraordinary animal friends. Now I get it! We are in Wonderland and I am Alice."

"No, my darling, this is real. In fact, it is more real than your other world. You are you, and this will never go away, not now or forever."

She blushed and they drank the wine and kissed a long, happy kiss, basking in the magical moment.

Tuesday morning, Meg and Silas drove over to the site where Raphael and his iguanas had created various stone samples for them to look at. Meg was so excited that she could hardly breathe.

At the site, Raphael stood to attention, saluting Meg and Silas, another cigarette screwed in the side of his mouth. Many of the iguanas were standing on their hind legs, waiting for her to decide which one she liked best.

"Wow guys, you really did it. These samples all look perfect." Meg ran her hand over them. "But I think I like this one best for the Theater and the main pair of apartment buildings (*Figure 20 – Stone #1*), and this one for the Library and the Sacred Arts Building (*Figure 21 – Stone #2*). This third one is perfect for Silas' house and the apartment building to its east, as well as the café and restaurant. Let's also use it for the apartment in front of the Library and the Sacred Arts Building (*Figure 22 – Stone #3*). The last one I like, which is rubble, is perfect for all of the retaining walls around the perimeter (*Figure 23 – Stone #4*). Thank you so much for this fine stonework."[21]

"Thank you, ma'am," Raphael said, bowing. Meg walked over and kneeled down beside him.

"You are my little prince now," she said, scratching him under the chin.

"Can I have another kiss?"

"Maybe next time, lover boy."

Meg approved the stone and made her way over to Silas who had left early to get the ATV started. Sitting there with the engine running, he was looking very Steve McQueen with his favorite pair of vintage tortoise Persol sunglasses on. "Good day dear, ready to go see the AutoCAD ants again?"

"Yes, can't wait!" replied Meg.

Meg had visited with the ants at least once a day for the last seven days. On the second, third, fourth and fifth days (*Figures 25* through *30*) she had sketched details on 3-D block-outs of the entire building compound that the ants had provided. Meg had also given the ants hundreds more hand-drawn details of every aspect of the buildings. Palladio, the head ant, would enlarge these sketches and details onto a large screen for all the ants to see.

Palladio was named after the sixteenth-century Italian Venetian architect, Andrea Palladio, for his design capability. After Meg told Palladio the details, he would then explain them to the architect ants, instructing which groups needed to incorporate each one of them into the design. Then, the ants would immediately go back to work.

On this eighth day of the ants' drafting schedule, Meg and Silas went to the Anthill to see the results. On the large screen, Pallad—as he liked to be called—projected each sheet of drawings and proceeded to explain them to Meg. She was astonished at the sheer mass of information they had produced. *How in the holy Hell had they done it? she wondered. And especially from just seeing sketches.*

Silas explained that the ants have profound and exceptional

intuitive abilities. "They can look at something and sense everything about it, and with architectural elements, they have trained themselves over these many years, with us as their tutors, to be especially good at this one discipline. In fact, we hire them out to architectural firms all over the world as Anthill & Company Architects, and people think that our ants are hardcore professional human geniuses." Pallad then presented Meg with surprise renderings (*Figures 31 & 32*) of the palace drawn by the ant artist extraordinaire, T. Scott Carlisle.

Meg sighed, "How is this all possible? All of this is just too much for me to comprehend. I'm exhilarated, happy and worried all at the same time!"

Silas smiled a closed mouth smile and then wisely put his hand on her hand. "Love, you worry too much. Just relax."

"Alright angel, you're right. You know, that's what people pay me to do."

"You mean people pay you to worry?"

She laughed, "In a way, yes. That way everything doesn't fall apart."

"Aww hell babe, now you got *us*. We take care of everything. No more worries. No more fears. Silas is here for you." The two Eskimo-kissed. Then, Silas led her to the door, tipping his panama estancia hat to Pallad on the way.

As they left, Meg turned to the ants and said, "You are all so amazing and talented. I love you all. And thank you T. Scott for these beautiful renderings. I will cherish them always."

T. Scott's black ant appearance suddenly turned red.

Outside Meg said to Silas, "Now that I have finally made a sketch of the Theater dome, which is the most elaborate of the stone roofs, I need to meet with the macaque monkeys to show them my designs for all of the roofs."

"I thought you'd never ask! Carlos told them to stay close in case we came over to see them. I will round them up now with my mind and we can go straight there for a meeting."

When they arrived, they saw Carlos enthusiastically talking to three monkeys. "Hey Magpie and Silly Silas! These are my buddies: Moe, Joe and Big Toe."

"Hi Meg, hi Silas. Show us what you got!" said Big Toe.

"Hi, my furry friends! The stone domes, barrel vaults, pitched roofs and flat roofs are all going to be built with the same stone as the walls. The iguanas will quarry it for you and will chomp it into the shapes and sizes we need. How does that sound?"

"That's groovy sister—when can we start?" said Big Toe.

"Hold your bananas, hot shots, let's look at my drawings so you can see what you'll be dealing with." She unrolled them. "Here is the crown jewel of the entire building: the Theater dome. It's a very old technique that I saw many years ago when I studied Spanish/Moorish architecture in the Andalusian region of Southern Spain. It involves intricately laid cut stone ribbing in a complex pattern that leaves a small circular space at the very top. The stone for the dome is then laid concentrically on top of this ribbing until it gets to the top. Here you will install a small dome made of glass stars held together with Roman cement. This entire structure will be the crème de la crème of the palace (*Figure 33*). Also, here is a sketch for a typical stone barrel vault where you will build these individual stone arches using keystone shapes, so they don't collapse. Then you will build the barrel vault (*Figure 34*) over wooden scaffolding that the other monkeys will have constructed already for your use. Can you do it? Can you build these?"

"What did you say? Can we do it? Does a monkey have a climbing gear? Of course, we can do it! Get those iguanas off their asses and get our stone cut, and we're off to the races!" Big Toe said.

"Wow, you guys sure are confident!"

Carlos said, "They have a lot of experience and can 'read'

any drawings you show them. They are the best I've ever seen. Smart, quick and highly skilled!"

"Okay guys, thanks for meeting with us. See you on site on the tenth day of construction for you to begin work on the Phase 1 buildings."

After Meg and Silas left, Moe said to the others, "Damn, that dome is some crazy, complicated shit. You guys sure we can pull that off?"

With a hand combing his chin, Carlos answered, "I think so. I know so. Maybe so. Hahahaha."

"Hey, that isn't very nice Carlos," Moe said, slapping him on the head.

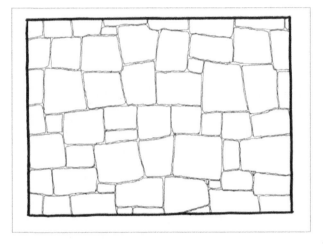

Figure 20 Stone #1

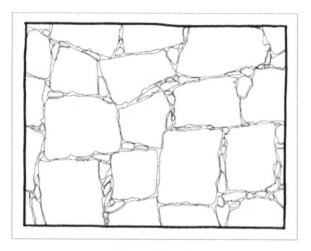

Figure 21 *Stone #2*

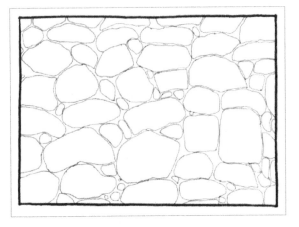

Figure 22 Stone #3

Figure 23 *Stone #4*

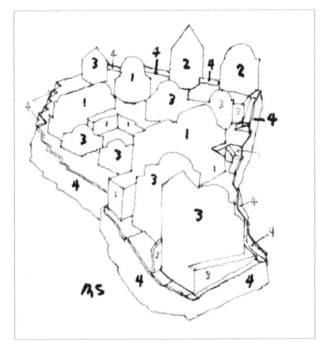

Figure 24 Locations of the four types of stone patterns

Figure 25 *Meg's sketches on 3-D models prepared by the Anthill*

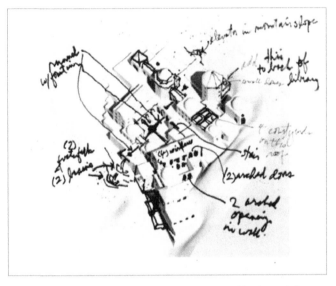

Figure 26 Meg's sketches on 3-D models prepared by the Anthill

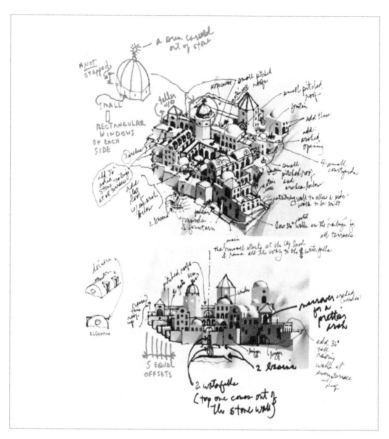

Figures 27 and 28 Meg's sketches on 3-D models prepared by the Anthill

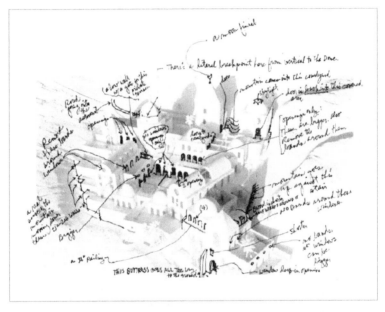

Figure 29 Meg's sketches on 3-D models prepared by the Anthill

Figure 30 *Meg's sketches on 3-D models prepared by the Anthill*

Figure 31 *A beautiful drawing by the ant artist extraordinaire, T. Scott Carlisle*

Figure 32 *A front elevation of the entire building compound by the ant artist extraordinaire, T. Scott Carlisle*

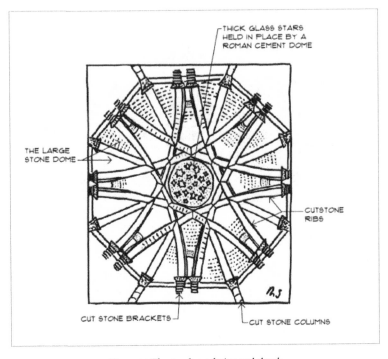

Figure 33 Theater dome design and sketch

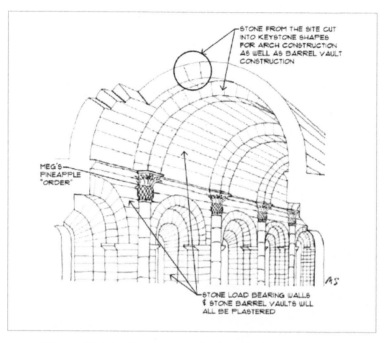

STONE FROM THE SITE CUT
INTO KEYSTONE SHAPES
FOR ARCH CONSTRUCTION
AS WELL AS BARREL VAULT
CONSTRUCTION

MEG'S
PINEAPPLE
"ORDER"

STONE LOAD BEARING WALLS
& STONE BARREL VAULTS WILL
ALL BE PLASTERED

Figure 34 *Meg's barrel vault construction sketch for the mason's monkey crew*

37

On Wednesday morning, Detective Rogers monitored the parking lot of the Hanalie Bay surf break for twenty minutes from his blue Jeep Rubicon while he ate a breakfast burrito and drank his morning coffee, black with no sugar. He was looking for any sign of the bozos that pulled off the heist. He was going to 86 that "Officer Donut" article if it was the last thing that ever happened to him.

Watching a few surfers head to the shore, an old red Chevy cutlass pulled up beside him and a dude with shoulder-length sun-bleached brown hair and no t-shirt hopped out. As he did, Rogers hollered at him through his Jeep window, "Hey dude, can you answer some questions for me?"

"Sure man, what's up?" The surfer leaned in on the windowsill of Rogers' Jeep.

"I'm a cop looking for a group of bad dudes. Any idea who can help me find them?"

He laughed, "Maybe, what you got for me, macho?"

"I'll give you a twenty?"

"Give me fifty and I might talk."

Rogers pulled out a hundred and forked it over to the surfer.

"Who you looking for? Lots of bad types around here. The wrong *moke* will throw any *haole* in a volcano if they look at his girlfriend wrong. The island is full of good vibes, but there are bad eggs around too. Meth-heads, crack dealers, whatever."

"The guys I'm looking for would be tough guys that steal shit for a living."

The surfer guy looked both ways shiftily, and then back at Rogers a little alarmed and said, "For real?"

"Yeah, what's it to you?"

"Hey man, don't tell them I told you, but this guy Red, an Aussie with a long scar on his cheek, is mean as hell when he's wave riding. Socked some freshman in the eye the other day for getting in his lineup. That's all I know."

"Okay, good, what's the kid's name who got punched? I'll toss you another big buck, kid."

"Alright, let's have it." Rogers pulled out another hundred and handed it over to the surfer. "Thanks bro—Ace."

"That's his name?"

"Yeah, like a sure card, he hangs around by the burrito stand near the pipe where all the girls are."

"Thanks dude."

"Yeah, later bro," the dude said, and got his board from the back of his convertible and jetted off towards the beach.

Wearing lime-green floral board shorts and a peacock-blue Quicksilver tank top, Rogers put on his tortoise Maui Jim shades and went to the beach to find Ace.

It wasn't hard. The nineteen-year-old, who was bigger than Rogers anticipated, was making the move on an older blonde surfer girl in a one piece, trying to get her phone number, but she kept teasing him by calling him "cute" and saying, she was "old enough to be his babysitter."

Rogers ordered an iced tea at In the Pipe Burritos and

waited for the girls to leave, then he walked over to Ace, who had a dark surfer tan and a typical surfer shag haircut—bangs and an overgrown mess in the back and around the sides. Rogers noticed the bruise around his left eye, the area still a little blue.

"You Ace?"

"Yeah, who's asking? You a *hodad*—a guy that hangs out at the beach, but doesn't ride?"

Rogers laughed, "No, I ain't no hodad, I ride the waves sometimes. Listen bud, I hear you're some kind of *jake* and got in the way of a lineup. Is that right?"

"Yeah! So what?"

"So, that guy who punched you is a bad dude and I need some information on him."

"What do you want?"

"I don't know, help me out. Who is he? What does he look like?"

"I don't know, man."

"I'll give you a fifty? You can buy a lot of burritos for your girlfriend over there."

"Alright mister, his name is Red and all I know is he has a big tat of Poseidon, that water god, on his right arm."

"Thanks bud." Rogers slipped him the fifty.

"Thanks 5-0." Ace took the fifty and wandered after the girl.

Rogers headed back to his Jeep and called the headquarters back in Lihue to search the police database for anyone named Red. Rogers assumed it was a nickname, but thought what the hell, he just might get lucky.

Sure enough, there was a Red Robinson in the system living right there on the North Shore of Hanalei Bay, just miles from that very spot. A couple of priors: one for shoplifting and one for drunk driving. Rogers scribbled down Red's address and sped off to go check out the house.

38

R ogers parked his jeep across the street from Red Robinson's A-framed bungalow tucked in between a massive array of tropical plants, with huge coconut palms soaring high into the sky all around the house.

He stuffed his mouth with a wad of strawberry-flavored Big League Chew bubblegum, a habit he had acquired after trading it in for his Wintergreen Skoal chewing tobacco a few years back. His wife had hated the disgusting habit and finally said, "That's it, it's me or the dip!" After taking a long look at their dog Spot—a bull terrier with a round brown spot around his eye—sitting beside him on the sofa, he thought about it for a moment and quit snuff forever.

Nothing much was happening at Red's. Rogers looked through his binoculars at the property, but the hedges were so thick he couldn't see anything. He checked his black Luminox Navy SEAL watch again, thought for a second about arranging a stakeout for the house, decided the paperwork would slow things down, set his binoculars down and hopped out to take a closer look.

He crossed the street and when he got to the driveway, he

peered down it. At the end of it was an open car garage, the view passing straight through to the blue ocean behind it.

Chewing his gum, Rogers walked around the perimeter. Finally, he discovered a path leading to the beach two houses down and took it. Making his way along the sand heading to Red's house, he stopped. From the beach, the back of the house was fully visible. He saw a large, gray rectangular porch. The lights were off in the house. No one home, he figured. He glanced around the beach and when he saw no one was looking, took the house steps up to the wide back porch. Peering in the windows, the living room and connecting kitchen resembled a normal rental, usually reserved for vacationers with bland black kitchen appliances and not much in the way of books. He tried opening the sliding door, but it didn't budge.

To his right, he noticed a rack of ten surfboards, "Bunch of dudes alright," he thought. Inspecting the surfboards, he observed they were all Arakawa sticks, custom made on the North Shore of Oahu. Leaving the house from the beach again, he made his way back to his Jeep. And he knew where he was heading.

———

THE NEXT MORNING, Rogers took a quick flight to Honolulu, rented a car and drove to the Waialua Sugar Mill Plantation on the North Shore of Oahu where he stopped at the Eric Arakawa Surfboard Factory. Walking in, he was greeted by a bro with a black trucker hat that read "ALOHA" in white letters. He asked him if Eric was around. Rogers knew Eric was a legendary shaper on the shores of Hawaii and had almost commissioned a board a long time ago. The dude said, "Sure, right this way boss."

Rogers was led into a white room full of fiberglass dust where Eric was finishing up a new white board. When he saw

Rogers, he stopped and took off his mask, "What can I do you for, boss?"

"Name is Rogers, I'm lead detective for the Kauai police. I need to ask you about some guys you shape for."

Eric looked concerned, "I don't know anyone I shape for really. Does this involve me?"

"Yes, it could. Tell me what you know about these thug surfers in Bernie's crew and I will leave you alone."

"Alright, give me ten." Rogers left the room to wait in the front office. Eric finished shaping the board, came out and said, "What's this all about?"

"Does a guy named Red Robinson ring a bell by any chance? He has a big scar on his face."

"No, not really. What do you want with me?"

"Get over it man and tell me what you know."

"Okay, okay, chill out. Yeah, yeah, I have shaped for him, Bern, Meat and Mug. Real losers if you ask me, but hey, they can surf a wave without getting wet if you know what I mean. Sometimes they even go ride Jaws in Maui, tow-in surfing. Gargantuan wave. You got to have big kahunas to ride that wave, if you know what I am saying."

"I see. Could you tell me where they hang out? I went by Red's house in Kauai to ask him some questions, but he wasn't home."

"I don't know man, right now I think those cats are hanging at Bern's place on Kauai. Got a word from a friend. Check out Little Italy Pizza there. That crew likes to grab a pie there and play the old Pac Man game in the corner."

"Alright man. *Mahalo*, friend."

"It's nothing."

39

On Wednesday evening, Silas sat in his low-slung chair in the cave with his right hand on top of the Touchstone. There, he gazed into the vastness of time, where he saw four rough men packing the Vortex's gold reserves into large black duffle bags in his house's below-ground vault. They were cackling like a bunch of mad hyenas. Next, they were standing right beside him in the cave and, for a moment, he could feel their presence, dark and gnarly like venomous snakes. They flashed a light on the Touchstone and when all four men placed their hands on it, a vision of black ravens covered the whole world. Silas wept, and the prescience of the men and ravens disappeared. Shocked, he sat still for another minute as a small tear fell down his face, and he inhaled the aroma of the wet rose oil that sometimes radiated from the stone.

He stood and exited the cave. It was a clear night and the white moon hung high in the sky. He knew he would have to prepare for the assault on the Vortex, but how? He couldn't let this interfere with the construction of Meg's building. It must go on. It had been his dream for the place now for over a century. He would instruct the animals and birds to help him with the thugs, but he did not want to endanger any of them. These thieves looked ruthless and would surely react violently to a bunch of animals attacking them.

BACK AT BERNIE'S HIDEOUT, The Pirate's Booty on Kauai, he and the three-man crew waited on Bug, betting on a cockfight on the outside land. One of the roosters, Buster, was oversized but kept getting dominated by Let's Get Busy, a little scrappy fellow.

When Bug drove up and walked over, the crew clanged their glasses full of Japanese whiskey, cheering his arrival. He informed them all about the property Mickey had vanished into.

"Good work Bug, tomorrow we'll take a chopper to surveil the area from above. Now come lay a bet down on Let's Get Busy and see if you can beat my bird," Bern said.

"Alright." Bug laid down a fifty.

40

The next day, the crew was packed into a rental chopper Mug was piloting high above Kauai, using the coordinates on Bug's phone to find the location. Meanwhile, Kahuna, Silas, Mickey, Meg, Eight Foot, Bane, Lono, Biscuit, Chloe and her friend Violet were packed into Mickey's truck and bed, rumbling down to the building site. Bob Marley's "*The Sun is Shining*" blasted from the speakers. The various animals, although they loved the beach, never dared go down to the cove and walk on two legs and talk. They had to protect their secret too: some passerby on a boat or helicopter might spot them.

Mickey parked and the crew bustled out wearing swimsuits and flip flops. Kahuna had a cooler full of frozen pineapple juice and a few pre-frozen margaritas. When the group passed through the main room of the underground cave, Silas hung back, letting them proceed to the beach.

He walked around inspecting everything, thinking pensively. He perceived by his inner sight that the men, when they came, would be arriving by boat. It was the only easy way into the property. Everything else was super secure.

At the gate to the beach, he figured he could affix a thin steel pipe between the door handle and the rock wall to keep the assailants from busting in. He thought about manning the entrance 24/7, but the power of the stone allowed him to perceive that the thieves might kill that person, and the rod would be enough.

Feeling satisfied with the solution, Silas left and walked out onto the beach, smiling. He kicked off his leather slides and dashed into the sand, tackling Meg to the ground where he tickled her.

Mickey kept eyeing Chloe, who just adored him.

A quite fit shirtless Bane hustled over and laid down on his towel beside Mickey.

"Hey bud, you know Chloe likes you."

"I know, I know."

"Well, what are you so afraid of man? Go on, ask her out."

"Well, I would, but maybe she likes me too much, you know."

"Hey, your loss man. What about that Anna chick at the health food store in town, did that never pan out?"

"Naw." He paused for a minute, watching Chloe laugh. "Hey, maybe I will ask Chloe out. She's looking pretty cute today."

"Yeah man, take her to the waterfall or something cool like that."

The whole group swam in the ocean with Biscuit, who loved frolicking in the waves, washing off the black dirt from the property that hid under his swollen belly. It was a perfect Hawaiian day, the kind pictured on postcards—the sun a magical blossom of orange.

Mickey flirted with Chloe by stealing her trucker cap and putting it on backwards.

At that moment, a chopper skirted around the edge of the

island above the group enjoying the sea. Kahuna thought it must be the Alcohol, Tobacco and Firearms (ATF) group.

"Oh hey, it's the man looking for *pakalolo!*" Kahuna said, pointing at the chopper while laughing. The ATF was always flying over Hawaii looking for fields of illegally-grown marijuana.

Through the binoculars, Bernie saw the group hanging out on the beach. "There, that amazing private cove has got to be the foot of the property. We will enter there. Those must be the owners." Bug grabbed the bird-finders from Bernie and looked. Seeing Mickey lying on the beach, he commented, "Yep, that's the surfer I saw alright, bunch of crazy hippies."

"That's it then, we will enter down there soon."

"Wahoo!" Meathead hollered.

Down below, Mickey reclined on a sea turtle towel, leaning up on his elbows and drinking his margarita while watching Chloe and Violet.

Meanwhile, Silas performed his slow, controlled Qi-Gong movements over by the massive northern rock that jutted far out into the ocean. He sensed the chopper wasn't looking for weed but was related in some way to his vision the other night. It was time to make the preparations.

Kahuna belly-flopped in the ocean, then he and Eight Foot tossed a Frisbee, while Chloe and Violet continued sunbathing.

Watching Silas perform his movements from the shore, Meg knew he was the one her heart had been calling for. She waded out into the surf and went swimming in the blue ocean for a while. In the distance, five dolphins popped up out of the water in unison, the sun reflecting off their shiny noses as they crested through the air.

After they were tan from the island sun—their hearts full of joy and love for each other and the earth—they left. As they passed through the iron gate, Silas waited and closed it behind him. He went and retrieved a metal fire prodder by the big earthen fireplace and returned. It looked like Poseidon's trident, and Silas felt good with it in his hand—like he was master of his own fate. He lodged it in between the door and the side wall of the cavern and followed the group, where they waited for him in the belly of the cave.

"What were you doing, Silas?" Eight Foot asked.

"Nothing, just working on the lock to the gate, that's all." He didn't want to alarm anyone.

They took turns riding the elevator back up to the property (groups at a time).

THAT NIGHT, Mickey cut a coconut with a machete and handed it to Chloe, whose eyes twinkled like little stars. He then cut another for him and the two walked into the forest. They sat down beside a tree, leaning up against it.

"It's good, isn't it?" Mickey asked her.

"Oh yeah, surfer boy." She took a big sip. "I want to talk to you, Mickey."

He moved in and kissed her steamily, holding her neck with his right hand. She smiled and they kissed some more. "What about?" he said.

"Who cares," she said, and they kissed again. In a moment, they were half-nude, making love on the cool dirt with the forest all around them.

Back at the main house, under the covers, Meg and Silas laughed together with Biscuit on the bed tickling their necks and heads with his nose like an Italian pig snorting for truffles. In the distance, not a sound could be heard down below on the shores of Kauai, which lay still in the cool night.

41

The first day of construction was Friday, October 29th (*Figure 35*). Meg could hardly stay in bed. She woke before dawn and showered, dressed and jumped on Silas, "Get up, get up you stud—today is like Christmas to me!" Silas woke up and she got off him and spun around the room with arms held out, head to the sky, smiling, "Today is the first day of the rest of my life!"

"You're right, babe, it is. You go on down to the site while I get us some of that incredible coffee Kahuna serves up."

"Sounds good honey."

Meg ran down to the site and could see that even though the sun was just cresting over the horizon in the distance, the iguanas were already there and the building area, which was normally stone gray, was now lizard green. There were iguanas everywhere preparing for the week ahead. They had received the Anthill's final set of working drawings and were busy reviewing the details for today's work. "Well, they may be iguanas, but they're early birds," Meg said aloud.

At the coffee stand, the sun was now up and Mickey, Chloe,

Bane, Lono and Kini were all waiting for Silas to get his morning cup.

"Hey guys!"

"Hey there Silas, ready for Day 1? I got my cooler," Bane said, showing off his old Igloo.

"Of course, I'm always ready for the day. Glad you brought some refreshments—we'll need them! It's a hot one."

"What will it be today Silas?" Kahuna asked.

"Same old same old. Actually, make it two. And let's make them Cuban buccis by dropping some sugar in those espressos."

"Sugar? You never eat sugar, boss!" Kahuna said.

"I know, but...today is the first day of the rest of our lives, boys. You won't believe it, standing there watching those little green fellas work. It's amazing!"

"I bet," Chloe said. "Let's go, I can't wait any longer."

Silas smiled, showing his teeth as Kahuna served him the Cuban buccis. He took his back in one long sip and said to Kahuna, "Come on big man, you're coming with us too. It wouldn't be a day without you!"

"Awesome," Kahuna said. Then, he wiped his hands on a bar rag, removed his work apron, and walked around the bar to join the crew.

In front of the assembly, Carlos was meeting with Raphael and his head crewmembers. Meg said hello and sat down to watch while she waited for Silas to arrive. In a few minutes, he showed up with their friends and her coffee.

"What's going on?" Silas asked Meg.

"It's like watching a play or a ballet with these guys. It's just so amazing!" she said.

"I know, watch them when they really get started," Silas said as he sat down.

Mickey and Chloe walked over to Meg and the two sat on a

quilt spread over the grass beside her. Then, Bane, Lono, Kini and Kahuna took a seat on the other side of them.

At that exact moment the iguanas went from what appeared to be random movements to the most precise and organized activity she had ever witnessed. This made the excavation work seem like child's play. Giant stone blocks were quickly and systematically being carried from the storage site down into the bottom of the giant holes for each building in Phase I. These were the foundation stones. Within hours, she and Silas could see all of the buildings taking shape. A few more hours later, and thick stone basement walls were standing. Raphael looked like a mad man (well, a mad iguana at least), running from here to there directing the green assembly. This was a far greater show than the excavations.

"I'm actually watching my design being built before my very eyes. I see it happening, but I don't believe it. Silas, pinch me to see if I'm dreaming."

Silas put his arm around Meg and said, "Isn't it the most wonderful sight to see these extraordinary reptiles building your beautiful masterpiece? Get used to it love, because this is your new reality. I hope you can handle it!"

"I can, I can—and I will, I will. You had me at my 'new reality!'"

When the day ended at exactly six p.m., all of the basement foundations and walls were complete. Meg, Bane, Lono, Kini, Chloe, Mickey and Silas called out to Raphael thanking him for a great day's work.

"Don't thank me, thank the team," Raphael said.

"Of course, a big mahalo to all of our beautiful iguanas! We'll see you all tomorrow bright and early!" Silas said.

Phase 1

Masons: Iguanas	①	2	3	4	5	6	7	8	9
Domes & Barrel Vaults: Macaque Monkeys	10	11	12	13	14	15	16	17	18
Timber framers: Rhesus Macaque Monkeys	19	20	21	22	23	24	25	26	27
Plumbers: Groundhogs	28	29	30	31	32	33	34	35	36
Electricians: Squirrels	37	38	39	40	41	42	43	44	45
Air conditioning: Mice	46	47	48	49	50	51	52	53	54
Plasterers: Orangutans	55	56	57	58	59	60	61	62	63
Cabinetry: Chimpanzees	64	65	66	67	68	69	70	71	72
Painters: Toucans	73	74	75	76	77	78	79	80	81

Figure 35 *Phase 1, Day 1 schedule*

42

A t approximately six a.m. on Day Two (*Figure 36*), Meg and Silas were right there perched on their same viewing spot ready for the day's activities to begin. Today, they brought folding chairs and a cooler full of iced lemonade, ham and cheese sandwiches on artisan wheat with handmade mayonnaise and heirloom tomato slices. It was the greatest show on earth—like a circus, but not really.

Carlos had already told them that the iguanas would be completing the first-floor walls today, as well as the Theater's tall walls since it only had one floor. Meg had been trying to resolve the Theater's cornice design but still had no revelations. Today was D-day. She would need to let Carlos know.

Meg loved construction sites, especially when they were hers. But this one, in particular, she felt overwhelmingly connected to. She had envisioned that the buildings would appear to rise out of the mountain and now she was getting to witness that, both literally and metaphorically.

Many years ago, Meg had learned that if she sat still on her construction sites, as well as off to the side of all the building activity, that she could feel and hear the *building* speak to her—

maybe not so much the building as the materials. She used only natural materials because they seemed to resonate with a certain energy that was tangible. They spoke to her—the stone told her how it wanted to be laid; the roof tiles did the same; the plaster told her how its surfaces wanted to feel the human touch; windows spoke to her of proportions, views and breezes; doors, of passages and time; wood beams and columns spoke to her of their strength and longevity.

Today, she sat on the site until she became empty. The ocean breezes, the salt air, the energy from the Touchstone all transported her mind somewhere else...a daydream perhaps... or was she actually there in another life? She's on a coast somewhere in Spain, it seems. She's a man, a worker, a stone mason. He's laying stone. He's strong and confident. He's surrounded by a hundred others, all doing the same. They are on wooden scaffolding. The stone is hoisted up to them by giant pulleys— massive pieces that have already been chopped and chiseled for placement, but he and the others must do the final chiseling for a perfect fit.

His father was a stone mason as was his father, and so on as far back as anyone could remember. He loved the feel of stone, its weight and textures. He felt alive and part of the earth as he handled it and fit it into a wall. The stones seem to speak to him as if he was one with them. When the buildings were being built and he arrived each day for work, he saw the team's handiwork, and was pleased. As the structures got further and further along he saw the architect's vision and was amazed to see how the stones he laid with his bare hands could transform into a sacred building. A church. He loved being a part of that.

Suddenly, Meg awoke from her daydream by the very real vision of a detail she had been pondering. It was the stone cornice detail at the roof's edge (*Figure 37*). She could see how it should be designed, carved, and laid in her mind—as clear as day.

Meg had learned over time to never chase a detail, but to allow it to enter her waking mind through her subconscious. Perhaps this was a detail she had designed as an architect or even laid as a stone mason in a former life.

Phase 1

Masons: Iguanas	1	②	3	4	5	6	7	8	9
Domes & Barrel Vaults: Macaque Monkeys	10	11	12	13	14	15	16	17	18
Timber framers: Rhesus Macaque Monkeys	19	20	21	22	23	24	25	26	27
Plumbers: Groundhogs	28	29	30	31	32	33	34	35	36
Electricians: Squirrels	37	38	39	40	41	42	43	44	45
Air conditioning: Mice	46	47	48	49	50	51	52	53	54
Plasterers: Orangutans	55	56	57	58	59	60	61	62	63
Cabinetry: Chimpanzees	64	65	66	67	68	69	70	71	72
Painters: Toucans	73	74	75	76	77	78	79	80	81

Figure 36 Phase 1, Day 2 schedule

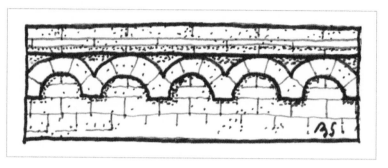

Figure 37 *Meg's vision for the Theater stone cornice*

43

On the tenth day of construction (*Figure 38*), the iguanas went right to work on the excavation for Phase 2 immediately—while the macaque monkeys started on the stone roofs for the Phase 1 buildings. They already had their drawings from the Anthill, so at six a.m. the frenzy, although organized, started.

As they chomped on the stone, holes started to appear, then stacks of stone emerged on the Phase 3 area. Meg and Silas both enjoyed this part of the show, reveling in how the stone stacks seemed to appear out of nowhere.

"This is more fun than a barrel-of-monkeys!" She knew right away that was a no-no, a gaff, a big fat foot-in-the-mouth.

"Now honey—you know better than that. What if our monkey friends said, 'That's more fun than a barrel-of-people?'"

"Hahahah, I'm sorry. Old sayings die hard. You know I love our simian friends," Meg said as she looked out at the exquisite workmanship by the macaque on the construction of the Theater's steep stone roof.

At the end of Day Ten, hundreds of neat stacks of stone and

perfect excavation holes existed. Meg looked on in wonder as the first phase of raw stone building shapes formed beautiful framed openings to the new excavations, the rest of the site and views of the ocean below. She always saw beauty in such things. Often, she wished that different stages of construction could be frozen in time to appreciate their raw beauty.

Phase 1

Masons: Iguanas	1	2	3	4	5	6	7	8	9
Domes & Barrel Vaults: Macaque Monkeys	(10)	11	12	13	14	15	16	17	18
Timber framers: Rhesus Macaque Monkeys	19	20	21	22	23	24	25	26	27
Plumbers: Groundhogs	28	29	30	31	32	33	34	35	36
Electricians: Squirrels	37	38	39	40	41	42	43	44	45
Air conditioning: Mice	46	47	48	49	50	51	52	53	54
Plasterers: Orangutans	55	56	57	58	59	60	61	62	63
Cabinetry: Chimpanzees	64	65	66	67	68	69	70	71	72
Painters: Toucans	73	74	75	76	77	78	79	80	81

Phase 2

Masons: Iguanas	(10)	11	12	13	14	15	16	17	18
Domes & Barrel Vaults: Macaque Monkeys	19	20	21	22	23	24	25	26	27
Timber framers: Rhesus Macaque Monkeys	28	29	30	31	32	33	34	35	36
Plumbers: Groundhogs	37	38	39	40	41	42	43	44	45
Electricians: Squirrels	46	47	48	49	50	51	52	53	54
Air conditioning: Mice	55	56	57	58	59	60	61	62	63
Plasterers: Orangutans	64	65	66	67	68	69	70	71	72
Cabinetry: Chimpanzees	73	74	75	76	77	78	79	80	81
Painters: Toucans	82	83	84	85	86	87	88	89	90

Figure 38 Day 10 of construction schedule

44

That evening, the crew of four thugs—Mugshot, Bernie, Red and Meathead—began loading their Wako fishing boat at Bernie's hideaway with black duffle bags full of supplies. Dressed in different shades of drab colors, they drove Bernie's Ram 2500 diesel truck down to Hanalei Bay, towing the Wako. There, they pushed off into the moonlit water.

With Meathead driving, the gruesome crew cruised the boat south along the West Coast of the island towards the Napali coast with nothing but a spotlight to guide them.

Not a person was in sight along the shoreline of the rugged and untamed Napali shoreline. The men had their spearfishing gear with them, operating under the guise of a night-fishing trip in case the Coast Guard stopped them. The water was choppy, and a few wild bumps almost sent Mugshot at the front flying into the water.

After fifteen minutes, the crew approached the secluded private cove of the Vortex, the moon hitting its sand with a pearly white luminescence. They killed the main engine and the light, and flipped on the trolling motor. Guiding their boat quietly close to the shore, they anchored. One by one, they piled off the boat. Meathead handed the three duffles to Mugshot who walked them over to the beach. Red was out already, inspecting the rock wall and looking for some kind of entrance. To the left of the stone wall, he found the arched manmade hole—inside of it stood an iron gate.

By the light of the moon, Red tried opening the door, but it was locked. "Give me the flamethrower, Meat," he demanded.

Meat looked in the bag, but the thrower wasn't there. Someone had forgotten to pack it.

"What the hell?" Meat said.

"What is it, you dolt?" asked Red.

"I don't know, it's not here. It's straight up missing."

"You forgot to pack it?"

"Don't tell *me* about it! That was Mug's job."

"You asshole!" Red said and slapped Meat's black ballcap down over his face. "Whatever, work on the lock, Bern."

Bern retrieved his welding supplies, walked up, pushed a welding shield over his eyes, kneeled down and began cauterizing the lock with a small welding tool. When the lock was toast, he pushed the iron handle of the door down, but it wouldn't budge. "I don't get it, we cooked the lock, but something is blocking the door from opening," Bernie remarked.

Red looked through the bars, closely examining the other side where he saw the pipe, lodged forcibly in between the door lock and the rock wall. He shook the metal gate with all his might, but no amount of force made it budge. Looking through the bars, he imagined mountains of gold waiting for them somewhere on the other side, and his heart grew wickedly cold. In a state of complete madness, he shook the bars again with all his fury, yelling.

At that moment, a bright light illuminated the beach and the crew spun around, squinting into the glare. It was the US Coast Guard. They just so happened to be patrolling the area that night looking for a couple who went missing on their catamaran. When they spotted the Mako anchored near the beach, they grew suspicious.

"Aw it's the bully man," Red said.

"What you doing here, boys?" Coast Guard officer Jake Smith asked as the boat drifted to shore. He hopped into the water and walked over with a spotlight shining on the disheveled crew of grunts.

"We was just out for a swim, nothing much," Meathead said.

Smith chuckled. "Doesn't look like much of a swim here, boys."

Officer Ray Nestle stepped off the Coast Guard boat onto the Mako, where he proceeded to flash his light in the boat.

"Got any yayo?" Smith asked the men.

"Naw, nothing like that," Meathead said.

Ray stepped off the Mako into the water and waded over to the shore where he walked towards the gate, shining the light on Bern's gear, which was strung all over the sand, then commented, "Smith, these boys are up to no good. Got welding shit here. I think you need to take a look."

Smith drew his gun swiftly and held it on Red, who raised his hands up in surrender. "Alright pretty boy, that's enough, take it easy," Red said to him.

Meathead, who was closer to the beach, made a quick swim for it the moment Smith drew his weapon. The commotion of him splashing caused both officers to turn fast. When they did, Red drew his Glock and fired a shot at Officer Smith, which hit him square in the right arm, wounding him. Smith fell to the ground in pain, his blood staining the sand burgundy.

Nestle spun back around, grabbing his pistol, but the other two men had him surrounded now and even Meat was making his way back to the shore.

"Look, don't hurt me, I got a family...three kids and a wife," Nestle said.

The crew jumped on him, and Meathead began stuffing his face into the sand like he was kneading a loaf of bread. "Get the boat moving Mug," Meat yelled.

Mug waded out to the Mako, while Red, Bern and Meat cuffed Nestle's hands behind his back with his own cuffs. They left him lying there on the beach where he was forced to endure Jake's screams piercing the night air.

The three men discussed a forced radio call by one of the officers to the Coast Guard at gunpoint in order to continue the heist, but there was no clear way into the property—besides, it was getting late now. In the boat, Mug bellowed for them to get in with him, so they could leave. They agreed and hopped into the purring Wako, pushing off into the blackness and leaving the two officers disengaged on the shore.

Nestle somehow managed to his use his left hand to turn on his smart watch and dial the office via voice command. When Howard at the front desk answered, Nestle yelled for him to send back-up to the Napali coast and look for their boat anchored in the beautiful cove. Twenty minutes later, two police boats arrived, finding the wounded officer and Nestle cuffed on the shore.

Police Officer Jim Flush quickly uncuffed Nestle and brought him on his boat to chase after the thieves.

"Which direction did they go?"

"North, that's all I know."

A few officers on the other police boat loaded Jake into their boat gently in order to take him to the hospital. "You're going make it, boss. Hang tight," one of the men said.

Heading north in a blaze of fury, the four bandits were speeding as fast as the Mako could haul. One police boat was following them, but the officers didn't have the crew in sight— in fact, they were miles away now.

45

I n the night, Silas woke at the Vortex, sensing danger was at hand. He moved without waking Meg from the Tower bed down to his reading room, where he lit a few candles and waited in silence by the soft yellow light.

Minutes later, Officer Neighbors called him asking to enter the grounds. Silas blew out the candles and reluctantly opened the gate for him and his partner.

The officers informed him about what had happened, and although Silas had experienced the foresight, he was still shocked. The police looked all around the main house and then asked to be taken to the beach where the incident occurred. On the way, Silas psychically warned Raphael and the iguana team that they were coming. By the time Silas and the cops neared the site for *Ha'alulu Maikai'i*, the iguanas had completely covered the entire structure, keeping it a secret. In the dark night, the palace was camouflaged by the green of the reptiles' bodies. Silas then guided the officers down to the cove.

Although the iguanas weren't concealing anything illegal, a property such as this would invariably draw the most unwanted attention to their community at this time—a time when Silas was still trying to figure out what to tell the world about the amazing building...if and when it ever came knocking.

Inspecting the beach, Neighbors asked, "What were those guys doing down here? I mean, what would they want with your little group?"

"Beats the hell out of me," Silas said. "Listen, how would you like to stay for a while here with us? I can make you some durian and a coconut."

Neighbors laughed and then said, "No, but thanks anyway."

After snooping around, taking evidence samples and photographs, the two officers left, passing by the foothills of the iguana-covered palace once again without even noticing it.

46

H aving arrived back in Kauai from Honolulu earlier that day, Rogers followed Eric Arakawa's tip and headed straight for Little Italy Pizza. There, he got to talking to one of Silas' friends—Bob, the owner. Every now and then Silas loved to go to Little Italy and order a dozen of their amazing deep-dish extravaganzas and take them back to the crew at the Vortex for a movie night. It was a break from the community's whole foods diet.

Of course, Bob knew Bern; they were pizza addicts and came in religiously.

"Where do those guys stay at?" Rogers asked.

"Up the hill just around Sunshine Gateway. The leader of the group, Bern, has a stupid stone sign that reads 'The Pirate's Booty' out in front of this massive spread of land. Got a house up there. I hear they even fight chickens sometimes. Not for the faint of heart. Go see."

THE ASSAILANTS PULLED into Secret Beach up the coast and anchored sideways as close to the shore as possible, in a little nook where a rock cropped out into the ocean. They grabbed their guns and bags and, leaving the boat, stormed the beach.

Ten minutes later, the police boat sailed right past the rock at Secret Beach that concealed the Mako.

After some time, the group made their way back on foot, attacking a man in a black Dodge Charger at a traffic light in town. After throwing him out on the pavement, they drove the car back to their place.

On the road outside, Rogers spotted the car as it sped around the corner so fast it almost flew off the road.

The local police had gotten a tip from a guy that four mean surfers he recognized from the beach had stolen his car. The group had an ill reputation as misfits, and the guy knew where they stayed.

In a minute, Rogers got out of his car and ducked in the forest around Bern's house, watching the property through some bird-finders.

Shortly, six squad cars with their lights on pulled into the driveway. The crew of four bandits were so tired, they had little left for a shootout. They surrendered to the massive police enforcement that surrounded the compound on all sides. "That's what happens when you shoot a Coast Guard officer," the arresting officer told Bern, who spat in his face right afterwards.

While they were being arrested, Rogers emerged. The gang was quietly pegged to the attempted break-in and shooting on the beach. Rogers spoke to the arresting officer, informing him he was almost certain these boys were also the gold-store thieves.

"Really? These losers?" Officer Dunford said.

"Yep, we think so. If you can, let's do a search here first for the missing gold. If it's not here, I am willing to bet it's at Red Robinson's A-frame house on the beach of the North Shore. Once we can get a warrant for it, I'll send my boys over to see if we can search it."

47

The Wednesday morning of November 3rd, Chief Riley and a squad of police cars arrived at Red Robinson's A-Framed beach house with a warrant. After breaching the door, they proceeded to carefully comb over the house.

In less than twenty minutes, they found the basement vault.

Getting into it was another story. A skilled safe-cracker on the squad's payroll opened it within an hour, revealing the stacks of gold bullion. Not to mention, they uncovered mountains of banded cash from previous heists, diamond necklaces and other rare jewelry the thieves had stolen over the years. Chief Riley and the Kauaian police department would ultimately link the thieves to three other major jobs on the island alone.

On Saturday morning, relaxing on his porch with a crisp newspaper headlined "Officer Rogers Strikes Again", Rogers ate a plain gourmet glazed donut and sipped his Starbucks venti coffee, smiling while he read the article detailing his capture of the thieves and recovery of the six hundred ounces of gold from their island hideaway.

The Vortex got a mention in the paper briefly regarding the thieves, but nothing about the palace or it being a secret community leaked out. And the FBI never came knocking. Silas and the group were able to retain their anonymity.

48

On Day 24 of construction (*Figure 39*), the iguanas were almost finished with the walls for the Phase 3 buildings, and the stone roofs were complete on Phase 1 and half complete on the Phase 2 buildings. But when Meg looked out from her mountain perch with Silas sitting quietly by her side, she saw visions of excavations of ancient buildings that had been buried by time and nature. She had the sense that they were uncovering buildings she had designed in another lifetime. She suddenly realized that she was in Peru at Machu Picchu, as one of the architects working directly under the High Priest. She and the other human architects were directing a crew of iguanas and monkeys to build the stepped terraces and buildings. She was a he, and he was amazed at the level of precision the animals could achieve in a short period of time. No human could ever install giant pieces of cut stone so perfectly beside other pieces of stone so tightly that no mortar was needed. Their ancestors had trained all of the birds and animals to work for them in every trade. Suddenly, it dawned on Meg that there was a Touchstone also in Peru, buried deep in a cave. Over several generations, the results of the team's work was beyond human comprehension. The architect told the animals what they wanted, and the animals understood. The High Priest directed the architects' work through his mind, along with the help of the stone.

Silas said, "Are you okay, Meg?"

She awoke and said, "Oh, I am sorry." She paused. "I just had the most amazing daydream."

"Were you dreaming or waking up?"

"Both."

"Well, go on, what was it you saw?"

"Another Touchstone, in Peru? Tell me Silas, are there more?"

"Ahhh, I don't want to upset you, but yes, there are three other ones just like the one here."

"Where are the others outside of Peru?"

"Iceland, South Africa and our stone."

Phase 1

Masons: Iguanas	1	2	3	4	5	6	7	8	9
Domes & Barrel Vaults: Macaque Monkeys	10	11	12	13	14	15	16	17	18
Timber framers: Rhesus Macaque Monkeys	19	20	21	22	23	(24)	25	26	27
Plumbers: Groundhogs	28	29	30	31	32	33	34	35	36
Electricians: Squirrels	37	38	39	40	41	42	43	44	45
Air conditioning: Mice	46	47	48	49	50	51	52	53	54
Plasterers: Orangutans	55	56	57	58	59	60	61	62	63
Cabinetry: Chimpanzees	64	65	66	67	68	69	70	71	72
Painters: Toucans	73	74	75	76	77	78	79	80	81

Phase 2

Masons: Iguanas	10	11	12	13	14	15	16	17	18
Domes & Barrel Vaults: Macaque Monkeys	19	20	21	22	23	(24)	25	26	27
Timber framers: Rhesus Macaque Monkeys	28	29	30	31	32	33	34	35	36
Plumbers: Groundhogs	37	38	39	40	41	42	43	44	45
Electricians: Squirrels	46	47	48	49	50	51	52	53	54
Air conditioning: Mice	55	56	57	58	59	60	61	62	63
Plasterers: Orangutans	64	65	66	67	68	69	70	71	72
Cabinetry: Chimpanzees	73	74	75	76	77	78	79	80	81
Painters: Toucans	82	83	84	85	86	87	88	89	90

Figure 39 Day 24 of construction schedule

Phase 3

Masons: Iguanas	19	20	21	22	23	(24)	25	26	27
Domes & Barrel Vaults: Macaque Monkeys	28	29	30	31	32	33	34	35	36
Timber framers: Rhesus Macaque Monkeys	37	38	39	40	41	42	43	44	45
Plumbers: Groundhogs	46	47	48	49	50	51	52	53	54
Electricians: Squirrels	55	56	57	58	59	60	61	62	63
Air conditioning: Mice	64	65	66	67	68	69	70	71	72
Plasterers: Orangutans	73	74	75	76	77	78	79	80	81
Cabinetry: Chimpanzees	82	83	84	85	86	87	88	89	90
Painters: Toucans	91	92	93	94	95	96	97	98	99

Figure 39 Day 24 of construction schedule

49

On Day 37 of the construction on Phase 1 (*Figure 40*), Meg and Silas watched from their chairs as the squirrels brought their electrical equipment onto the site, neatly arranging it in the categorically appropriate stacks for its efficient use. As usual, this orderly work both impressed and astounded Meg since she had never witnessed any of this from humans—or at least the humans she had known. On the same day, the groundhogs were tirelessly installing plumbing pipes for the Phase 2 buildings. Over on Phase 3, the monkeys appeared to be wizards as they carried their already milled wood floorings into the buildings. Meg loved seeing every phase being worked on at different levels of development by different trades. She had never witnessed such a sight!

At six a.m. on the dot, the real activity suddenly started.

As before, Meg and Silas saw the piles of materials decrease quickly, as if in fast-forward, the squirrels carrying it all into the first Phase buildings. Silas and she quietly sneaked down and entered the Theater building to peek at the goings-on. The squirrels were everywhere on every wall—wires and conduits and such being installed. Vertical channels and chases (for the larger conduit) had been left in the stone walls by the masons.

Carlos was orchestrating it all with complete mastery, like the conductor of a symphony.

As they watched, squirrels could be seen scurrying in and out of every window and door opening, carrying supplies in and scraps of debris out—like a choreographed ballet. Simply beautiful! thought Meg.

"Silas, where does the power come from? There are no overhead power lines, transformers or even solar panels in sight anywhere here?"

"I'll show you. It's really neat. No one will miss us, that's for sure."

They went over to the elevator and Silas said, "There's another stop mid-way down to the beach, but its elevator button is hidden for security purposes." He touched the wall by the controls at some mysterious but exact spot and soon the lift stopped. When the door opened, they were in a vast cavern within the mountain. Meg could see a glow of light in the distance.

"What's that?"

"That, my dear, is our energy source. Let's go take a look!" When they approached the light, which was emanating from the east, Silas said, "My father discovered this cavern and the energy source here not long after working with the stone. It told him there was a profound vibration coming from deep within this part of the property."

"But what is it? I mean, how do you harness it and use it for electricity?"

"Well, we believe it is a very small version of what is at the core of our planet Earth. It's like a volcano, but it's not building up any pressure. It's basically the perpetual energy that humans have been searching for since the beginning of time. My father was himself an inventor and a scientist, and he had vast knowledge of power about steam, piping and turbines. Essentially, we have steam generators that will never run out!"

"Show me!"

"Okay." Silas opened a door nearby and they stepped into another giant cavern. This one had row after row of steam-generated turbines with pipes in unison leading from them into another room. In this room the energy was being converted to electrical power. Conduits were running from these engines straight up to where the Vortex was, as well as to the building site. Other conduits ran to the north and disappeared into tunnels, supplying electricity to the rest of the property.

Meg was amazed. "Well, I'll be damned. I have never seen anything to equal this. Silas, you never cease to amaze me!"

"As you do me, my love."

Phase 1

	1	2	3	4	5	6	7	8	9
Masons: Iguanas	1	2	3	4	5	6	7	8	9
Domes & Barrel Vaults: Macaque Monkeys	10	11	12	13	14	15	16	17	18
Timber framers: Rhesus Macaque Monkeys	19	20	21	22	23	24	25	26	27
Plumbers: Groundhogs	28	29	30	31	32	33	34	35	36
Electricians: Squirrels	(37)	38	39	40	41	42	43	44	45
Air conditioning: Mice	46	47	48	49	50	51	52	53	54
Plasterers: Orangutans	55	56	57	58	59	60	61	62	63
Cabinetry: Chimpanzees	64	65	66	67	68	69	70	71	72
Painters: Toucans	73	74	75	76	77	78	79	80	81

Figure 40 Day 37 of construction schedule

Phase 2

Masons: Iguanas	10	11	12	13	14	15	16	17	18
Domes & Barrel Vaults: Macaque Monkeys	19	20	21	22	23	24	25	26	27
Timber framers: Rhesus Macaque Monkeys	28	29	30	31	32	33	34	35	36
Plumbers: Groundhogs	(37)	38	39	40	41	42	43	44	45
Electricians: Squirrels	46	47	48	49	50	51	52	53	54
Air conditioning: Mice	55	56	57	58	59	60	61	62	63
Plasterers: Orangutans	64	65	66	67	68	69	70	71	72
Cabinetry: Chimpanzees	73	74	75	76	77	78	79	80	81
Painters: Toucans	82	83	84	85	86	87	88	89	90

Phase 3

Masons: Iguanas	19	20	21	22	23	24	25	26	27
Domes & Barrel Vaults: Macaque Monkeys	28	29	30	31	32	33	34	35	36
Timber framers: Rhesus Macaque Monkeys	(37)	38	39	40	41	42	43	44	45
Plumbers: Groundhogs	46	47	48	49	50	51	52	53	54
Electricians: Squirrels	55	56	57	58	59	60	61	62	63
Air conditioning: Mice	64	65	66	67	68	69	70	71	72
Plasterers: Orangutans	73	74	75	76	77	78	79	80	81
Cabinetry: Chimpanzees	82	83	84	85	86	87	88	89	90
Painters: Toucans	91	92	93	94	95	96	97	98	99

Figure 40 Day 37 of construction schedule

50

That night, the entire community was seated at two long tables covered with perfectly starched white tablecloths in the old fort café's main room, lit full of candlelight. The group was chatting amongst themselves about the building, commenting on the day's events while Miles Davis' "Round Midnight" played overhead.

Mickey came in through the door from the kitchen with the first tray of appetizers—he helped Chef Bojangles out in the kitchen on most evenings and tonight he had donned a white chef's coat with work shorts. He delivered the appetizer— "*Bojangles' Slap Ya Mama Gumbo*" with plump crabmeat—to each person, winking at Chloe when he set hers down. Banjo, the Chef's other helper, a lanky twenty-two-year-old with a long black ponytail and a Mediterranean nose, followed with the second tray of gumbo, while Mickey went back to retrieve the Creole Caesar Salads.

Not one for formality, Silas insisted everyone go ahead and start. After a few bites of tonight's gumbo, he commented that the roux was extra thick, just the way he liked it.

"I have never even been to New Orleans or had gumbo before," Meg said.

"Never had gumbo?" Silas said, astonished.

"No, this is my first."

"Well dive in and swim my dear. There's enough for seconds if you like."

Meg tasted it and said it was "otherworldly". Silas and the table laughed.

"It feels like we're walking down Royal Street to me, flipping a silver dollar into a worn-out open saxophone case. That's what it tastes like," Bane said.

"Yep, I can hear those old boys now, playing that jazz," Silas said.

"Nothing like the sax," Bane said.

Lono asked Meg, "So what day are you guys on and how's it going, Meg?"

"Well, it's going. I don't even know what day. My head is spinning. Don't get me wrong, *I love* to watch it, but I get nervous because of how fast they go. There's nothing like it in the whole world."

"It's like lightning in a bottle, right dear?" Silas asked.

"Yes, you could say that."

"Well, I have a little lightning in a bottle for you now, Megathon," Bane said, and started pouring her a glass of red wine out of a historic-looking bottle, the label peeling a little and the letters faded.

"No really, no...I'm not in the mood."

"Nope, not gonna hear it. This here is the ministry of health." Bane kept pouring a huge glass of wine.

"That's enough, really."

"Meg, you really should enjoy it, it's a very fine glass of wine," Silas said.

"I'm not a big wine enthusiast."

"Well, you will be after this glass, girl," Chloe said, holding up her glass. "It's the Chateau Cheval Blanc 1947."

"The French masterpiece," Bane commented, while corking the bottle.

"Well, okay, what's so special about it?"

"I'll tell you, Meg." Silas swirled his glass around and sipped it. "I hear it was very, very hot in this region of France on that particular year which yielded an uncanny wine, high in sugar, rich and porty...kind of like you. Cheers!" he said and the two clinked their glasses.

"Aw, that's sweet," Meg said. After sipping it she added, "It does taste special."

"It costs a pretty penny too, but we drink our money here when the weather is good on a night like this," Silas commented.

The group finished their appetizers, and Mickey and Banjo brought out two platters of perfectly boiled spiced shrimp—one for each table—along with some bowls of "*Bojangles' Dirty Grub*" (dirty rice: white rice cooked with the trinity of bell pepper, onion and celery, pork, cayenne and black pepper), a large serving plate stacked high with beef short ribs and a side of horseradish sauce.

Once the tables had cleared their plates, Chef Bojangles walked in and everyone applauded the giant green alligator.

"What a meal, Chef," Bane said, nodding to the gator.

"You really like the way I cook, old boy?"

"You know it."

"Well, look at me move," he said and started moonwalking on his reptile feet along the smooth wooden floors.

"Aw yeah Chef, get it!" Kahuna said.

Then, the Chef walked over to Meg. "How you doing tonight, gorgeous?"

"Good Bojangles, but the food was a little salty for my taste."

"What?" Chef said. Then Meg started laughing.

"Where's my treat?" she asked.

"Your what?" the Chef inquired.

"My treat! The other night, you said you would have a little something special for me, but I never received it. Well, where is it?" Meg asked again.

"Slow down girl, it's coming. Bojang-o didn't forget about you. Naw." Bojangles turned to Mickey and clapped twice. Mickey exited and came back out, rolling a trolley cart with a big pan on it, some bananas, a few sticks of butter, brown sugar, and a decanter full of Guatemalan dark rum.

"What is it?" Meg asked.

"You snooze, you lose," Silas said.

"Just watch girl, we gonna take you all the way down to Bourbon Street tonight, where the trolley carts don't lie. They hear all the secrets every night in the Crescent City."

"Okay, I'm waiting. Surprise me."

Bojangles headed over to the cart and turned on the flame.

"First we add the butter." He then proceeded to melt a whole stick of butter. "Then some brown sugar." He added it next.

"What are you trying to do, Mr. Bojangles? Kill me?"

"I am trying to make you come alive, girl. You need more passion in your life, and that's what cooking is all about. Just watch."

Once the butter and sugar had browned, Chef added in a little heavy cream, and cooked it for a second. Then he added in some sliced bananas.

"I am still waiting, Chef. It's like the slowest trolley ever."

"Alright alright, I got something for you, hotcakes. Hold your horses."

At that moment, the Chef poured in the dark rum, took a lighter out of his pocket and lit the pan. A huge flame ignited, bursting into the air; Bojangles wiggled his long tail while shaking the pan.

Meg clapped, "Wohoo! Now that was amazing, Chef."

"I would be lying if I said I didn't tell you so."

Mickey and Banjo walked up to the chef with two trays full of ice cream, and the caramelized bananas were placed on top of each bowl. "Get it while it's hot," the chef said.

When the bowls were served, Chloe and Meg dug in while the rest of the table and Bojangles waited for Meg's reaction.

"I dare say, it's heaven on a spoon," Meg commented.

Bojangles clapped and said, "Then, my work is done here, ladies and gents. Goodnight."

The assembly finished off the Cheval Blanc and uncorked a few more bottles. The obscene price tag of $304,000 was meaningless to everyone. The group laughed until their faces hurt. It was a night Meg would never forget; she knew she had found friends for a lifetime—people she could be herself with, and that was a treasure more valuable than all the gold in the world.

51

Monday, November 1st, Silas and Meg were taking a break from watching the construction. He was putting the final trim to the topiary of the two toucans rubbing their beaks together, magically in love. It was a masterpiece. Meg clapped in approval from the stone garden bench, where she sat with a book from the Library, wearing a wide-brimmed straw hat.

At that moment, she felt an awful sting on her foot.

"Ouch!" she cried out in displeasure and looked down to find a big, gnarly insect there.

Silas dropped the clippers and ran over to her. He carefully removed the six-inch-long spiky green caterpillar with his canvas garden gloves, and then he let the caterpillar go.

Meg's leg began reacting to the sting, swelling and turning bright red. She grimaced, grabbing the area with her hands.

"What the hell was that?" she pleaded.

"A stinging nettle caterpillar, dear Meg. They're poisonous. I think you're having an allergic reaction to the venom."

"Oh my, it feels like a gunshot wound."

"Best thing to do is to get drunk for three days on dark

rum," he said, smiling. She smiled back through her pain. "I am joking."

"Tell me, why on earth couldn't you stop him from biting me?"

"Well, these little venomous creatures can't hear me for some reason. We just can't figure it out. And they are dangerous as hell." Silas picked her up and carried her over to the main house to his bedroom.

He sat her down on the bed. Then he used some tape to carefully remove the caterpillar's nettles from her foot. Afterwards, he got a jar of water and began to wash the area.

"You will be well very soon, my dear. This water is special."

"Really? How so?"

"It's from our fountain, the Fountain of a Thousand Summers. Watch closely."

In a moment, her foot and leg began to look miraculously better, and the pain was gone.

"My leg feels better already. Ooh, Silas, that stuff is amazing. Can I have some more to drink?"

He chuckled. "Come my dear, let's go see it."

The two headed out down to the fountain, where Silas cupped his hands and drank the delicious water. Meg drank some of it too and in a moment, she was feeling very free and alive, like she felt after the coffee.

"This stuff is the nectar of the gods," Silas said, watching her.

"You can say that again, I feel so good now."

"Now tell me dear Meg, what do you think of our toucans?" (*Figure 41*)

"I think they look more like me than you."

"I don't think so," he said and they both laughed.

Figure 41 *Silas' Toucan Topiary garden*

52

On Day 53 of construction (*Figure 42*), it was almost the end of another nine-day building cycle, and there was a buzz going around the site, since the next day was going to be the halfway point for the construction of all the buildings. The mice, squirrels and groundhogs were all working away on Phases 1, 2 and 3 respectively. Actually, in just another forty-five days all of the structures would be complete.

Meg's mind was awhirl with thoughts about the process and Phase 4, which involved the courtyards, the remaining retaining walls, the paving, flights of stairs, fountains, runnels and of course all of Silas' plantings. He wouldn't share any of his layout or even plant materials with her, and that bothered her, but she knew that somehow it was for the best. She figured Silas had his reasons and he always seemed to be right. At the end of the day, she told him that she was tired and needed to rest, so she headed back to her room in the Tower.

Since arriving at the Vortex, Meg had experienced things no one else would ever experience—what a wild and joyous ride she had been on. Her mind had been liberated and her creative energy was at its peak. Furthermore, she was in love.

Now, lying there in bed, Meg drifted into a dream about her mother being in a violent car wreck. When she awoke, her heart was racing, her body wet with sweat. She could hear the glass breaking like she was right there in the car. Her mom was calling for her, "Meg! Meg! Help me! I'm bleeding!" Her first thought was: *I must go home now.*

She went down the hall and opened the door to Silas' reading room, where he was silently working. He always worked there early in the mornings when no one else was awake. "Hi, love," he said, and Meg told him about her dream, explaining that she just wanted to take a quick trip home to check on her mother after the nightmare.

"Okay, my love. Tomorrow, I will help you make the necessary arrangements."

She fell asleep that night peacefully, thinking about Silas' words.

However, Silas had plans of his own, and figured out how to send her home at once in his own special way. That night, he devised a potion to make Meg sleep and dropped it between her lips while she was deep under. Then, he carried her with her purse and cellphone up to the cave, to the Touchstone.

Arriving at the stone, he sat down, holding her body, which was deep in a trance from the magical herbs, and brushed her cheek with his thumb. He then placed his right hand on the Touchstone, which lit up with an aural light, filling the dark cave with a mystical energy. He thought about being in Meg's bedroom back in East Hampton with all his might. A moment later, he could see the room as clear as day in his mind's eye. While maintaining that vision, the energy from the stone began to envelop her body with violet-blue and golden light, sprinkled in dots of white light throughout the rays, like stardust. And in a moment, she vanished in the rapture of it all.

Phase 1

	1	2	3	4	5	6	7	8	9
Masons: Iguanas	1	2	3	4	5	6	7	8	9
Domes & Barrel Vaults: Macaque Monkeys	10	11	12	13	14	15	16	17	18
Timber framers: Rhesus Macaque Monkeys	19	20	21	22	23	24	25	26	27
Plumbers: Groundhogs	28	29	30	31	32	33	34	35	36
Electricians: Squirrels	37	38	39	40	41	42	43	43	45
Air conditioning: Mice	46	47	48	49	50	51	52	(53)	54
Plasterers: Orangutans	55	56	57	58	59	60	61	62	63
Cabinetry: Chimpanzees	64	65	66	67	68	69	70	71	72
Painters: Toucans	73	74	75	76	77	78	79	80	81

Phase 2

Masons: Iguanas	10	11	12	13	14	15	16	17	18
Domes & Barrel Vaults: Macaque Monkeys	19	20	21	22	23	24	25	26	27
Timber framers: Rhesus Macaque Monkeys	28	29	30	31	32	33	34	35	36
Plumbers: Groundhogs	37	38	39	40	41	42	43	44	45
Electricians: Squirrels	46	47	48	49	50	51	52	(53)	54
Air conditioning: Mice	55	56	57	58	59	60	61	62	63
Plasterers: Orangutans	64	65	66	67	68	69	70	71	72
Cabinetry: Chimpanzees	73	74	75	76	77	78	79	80	81
Painters: Toucans	82	83	84	85	86	87	88	89	90

Figure 42 Day 53 of construction schedule

Phase 3

Masons: Iguanas	19	20	21	22	23	24	25	26	27
Domes & Barrel Vaults: Macaque Monkeys	28	29	30	31	32	33	34	35	36
Timber framers: Rhesus Macaque Monkeys	37	38	39	40	41	42	43	44	45
Plumbers: Groundhogs	46	47	48	49	50	51	52	(53)	54
Electricians: Squirrels	55	56	57	58	59	60	61	62	63
Air conditioning: Mice	64	65	66	67	68	69	70	71	72
Plasterers: Orangutans	73	74	75	76	77	78	79	80	81
Cabinetry: Chimpanzees	82	83	84	85	86	87	88	89	90
Painters: Toucans	91	92	93	94	95	96	97	98	99

Phase 4

All Paving & Planting: Silas and his crew	100	101	102	103	104	105	106	107	108

Figure 42 Day 53 of construction schedule

53

W hen Meg awoke, she was miles and miles away in her bed at home in East Hampton. She jerked upright and looked down at the palms of her hands, wondering how on earth Silas had sent her home.

Falling back on her pillow, she said, "Think Meg, think. How did I get here? Was that all just a dream?" It really could have been. I mean, it *was* that strange, she thought.

But it wasn't, her skin was dark brown from the Hawaiian sun. And she was wearing the same clothes she had on in bed last night.

Getting out of bed, she took a hot shower. She was happy to be at home, and truthfully, there was nothing to complain about except that Silas and her new life were missing. She noticed her phone was in her pocket and her purse was on her bedside table, even though she hadn't used either in weeks. She tried turning the phone on, but it was out of juice. She plugged it in and waited for it to charge. In a few minutes, the screen lit up.

She dressed in her favorite uniform of a white shirt and khakis and got in her Mercedes. Still frightened by the dream of the car wreck, she called her mother to check on her. There was no answer. Meg was in a full panic now, thinking about the dream again; the sound of glass shattering in her memory, her mom calling out for her in terror, "Meg! Meg! Help me! I'm bleeding!"

She dialed the office next. Sam answered, "Hello, Summers & Company Architects, this is Sam."

"Sam, it's me, Meg! I am back now!"

"What? You're back? Break open the champagne!" he hollered.

"Yes, I was on a special assignment in the outback of Hawaii."

"Yeah right Meg, you can tell us all about your rendezvous with Mr. Hunk Away now. I am here, Peg is out for some supplies, Mal is in the back. Guess what?"

"What?"

"We did it. Somehow, we kept the ship going here without missing much of a beat. Your mom also managed to pay your electric bills with her spare key."

"Oh nice, thank you so much Sam. Hey, is she alright?"

"Scarlett? Yes, well, I mean she's very worried about you, but I just spoke to her this morning. She calls every day to check on you."

Meg breathed a sigh of relief. "Thank God! I had the worst dream last night that she was in a terrible car wreck."

"No, I mean, not that I know of."

"Okay, thanks, I will be there soon, ciao." When she said the Italian word, she remembered Raphael's sweet face saying it and almost cried. Then, she glanced in her rear view mirror and swore she saw Carlos driving the car behind her. He was all teeth and waved at her with his one free hand. She did a double take—looked away and back at the rear view mirror again—and realized her mind was playing tricks on her—that it was just a man dressed in a neat white button up shirt with a tie on his way to work.

At the office, when Meg walked in, Peg and Sam hugged her, crying. Hearing the commotion, Mal came in and gave her a gentle hug as well.

"Where were you girl for all that time? You were gone for so long!" Peg said.

"Let's just say I was on the assignment of a lifetime."

"Nice, any pictures?" asked Sam.

"Not yet, maybe never. It's that kind of thing. Super top secret." She put a finger to her lips. "So, what have you got for me Mal? How can we pick up where I left off right away and get down to some business?"

"Not much. Bob and I will fill you in," Mal said. "Come with me to my office."

54

The news of Meg's return sent thrills through her staff. All the architects in Manhattan Zoomed in to say hello and congratulate her for making it out alive from wherever she had been. She explained by saying she had needed a sabbatical.

Officer Henry called to take a statement from Meg, who told him she had run off to Hawaii to do a crazy assignment for an eccentric billionaire, and it was top secret.

Dawn, Scarlett and her good friend Sally showed up at the office that afternoon to see her. When Meg saw Dawn walk into her office, a smile broke out across her face. Her time in Hawaii had destroyed what was left of her prideful distaste for her sister. The two hugged, and Meg couldn't stop the tears during their embrace.

"I thought you would never forgive me, Meg."

"It's okay, it's all over now. No one even cares about it." A tear came to Scarlett and Sally's eyes as they stood in the door-way, watching the sisters hug.

"Aww, how sweet," Sally said.

"How are you doing Dawn, tell me? I want to know," Meg asked.

"I'm good now that I have you in my life again."

"Oh, congratulations girls, I just knew you would forgive her, Meg. There's nothing left to fight over anymore is there?"

"No, let's let bygones be bygones," Meg said.

And after that, the four ladies agreed to go out to eat dinner at a French Michelin 3-star restaurant overlooking the Atlantic that was all the buzz. Meg steered them to the liver pate appetizer instead of their usual foie gras for a change, explaining that she hated how the ducks were force-fed food to fatten their livers. She despised it even more after being with all her animal friends. Scarlett, Sally and Dawn listened carefully, instead of ignoring her like they used to when she brought up the subject. They all sipped iced gin and soda with lime twists and clinked their glasses to the good life.

"So where were you really Meg? Tell us? We just have to know," Sally said, removing her leopard-print jacket.

Meg smiled with pursed lips. "I was away. With a guy."

"No way! Where did you meet him?" Dawn asked.

"Who is he? Can I see him?" Sally asked.

"Well, I don't have a picture."

"You're so tan sweetie, were you somewhere warm? Tell us. We just have to know," Scarlett said.

Meg laughed. "Well, actually, I was really in Hawaii at a monastery with a vow of silence included, and not with a guy. That's where I was, and now you all know."

"I understand," Dawn said.

"Good for you, Meg. Smart to take care of yourself with the Lord," Scarlett said.

"I love yoga, did you get to do any yoga?" asked Dawn.

"Well, it wasn't that kind of monastery."

At that moment, the waiter arrived with their coq au vin on a tray; all women had decided to order the same thing—a ritual they had always done before Mick and the affair with Dawn. "Let's eat guys, we can talk about it later, over a bottle of wine when my mind has had a chance to rest."

"Okay, honey, it is your business after all," Dawn said, trying this time to truly respect Meg's affairs.

55

A fter dinner, Meg was standing in her empty kitchen, her back sore from sitting in the office chair all day. She had been doing so much walking and swimming in Hawaii, she didn't realize how lame and difficult sitting in that chair was.

She was so happy after reuniting with her family and Sally, but she also felt different, like something was missing. She picked up her phone to see if she had any new calls, hopefully one from Silas. But she had no number for him, and he would never call her either—that much was certain. She still couldn't figure out how she had gotten home. Probably the Touchstone.

And why had Silas sent her back? She was asking to go home that last day, but she didn't want to be cast away from the Vortex with no goodbye. The very thought of him caused her eyes to water. She wondered what he was doing. All of a sudden, she wanted to be there with him right away.

Depressed, she uncorked a bottle of Monterey Merlot and sat down in her king-sized bed alone, pulled up her MacBook Air and searched the internet for the Vortex.

The whole time she was at the community, she had never

left the property, not once. She had left the note with the geographic coordinates and address in her bedside table drawer at the Tower. If she returned, surely she could find the address again! What was it? 225 Palm Lane or something like that. Aw, shoot, she couldn't remember. It was a long drive in the Bronco that first day to the property. She vaguely remembered the way, but she wasn't sure she could guide a new driver back there. She decided to call the hotel where she stayed, inquiring after the driver's whereabouts. Lisa, the manager at the Cliffside Resort, said Earl had quit about a month ago. When Meg pressed for his phone number, Lisa told her she couldn't give out his personal information.

Frustrated, she spent over an hour on Google Images looking for the community, anything to catch a glimpse of the tranquil place she had called home, but there was nothing. Next, she searched Google Earth—Google's satellite imaging application, but the Napali coast was so big, she couldn't remember where to look.

The next day at work, she told Peg to hold all calls while she continued her search for the Vortex, but after some serious looking, she found nothing of any value on the net.

56

W ork resumed as normal. Everyone Meg worked with had forgotten that she disappeared for so long within a few weeks. Sam bought her a majestic bonsai tree that he placed on a stand in her office. He watered it for her, but the Japanese tree only reminded her of Silas and his garden.

Days piled onto days, which turned into weeks, which bled into months, all the while Meg kept searching the internet for the Vortex in her spare time. It was all she could think about. When she couldn't find a trace of the place online, she gave up the search, burying herself in her work like she always had. She tried to kill the memory of Silas and their building, but work alone couldn't get rid of it.

She needed to see the shores of Kauai again to feel complete.

57

In early March 2022, Meg attended a flashy Christian Dior gala ball in Manhattan and went stag, against everyone's suggestions. All the glitz, glamour and expensive champagne did little to cheer her up. Standing by the hors d'oeuvres table, Meg's ex-husband Mick Drewford walked up dressed in a black tuxedo with his long, dirty-blonde hair slicked back, carrying a champagne flute in his right hand.

"Hi Meg, where have you been all these years? I heard you went missing or something like that."

"Mick, it's you. I didn't expect to see you here. Listen, I don't want to talk about it. Not ever again."

"What? Let's just be friends, okay? I miss you."

"Mick," she said, half laughing. She was so unimpressed by him now. She reached down to fidget with her black sequin dress. "I don't do this. This friend thing. Leave me alone." She started to leave, but he blocked her move with his body.

"Hold up, listen! Let me get you a martini, okay? We can make it dirty."

"No, I gotta go. Move. You look stupid by the way," she said, and walked off.

The encounter with Mick and her memories of Silas made her so upset that when her stretch Cadillac Escalade limousine reached her posh Hamptons condo, she rushed inside to drown herself in a bottle of Pinot Noir.

Reclining in her black Eames chair with the sleeting rain outside the window, Sinatra's "I'll Never Smile Again" came on shuffle through the speakers. Moved to tears, she proceeded to listen to the whole "In the Wee Small Hours" album from Ole Blue Eyes, while polishing off the bottle. Just like Frank, she thought she could never love again after Silas...that he was her forever one.

Now drunk, she decided to search Google for the Vortex again.

Lo and behold, this time she came upon an image leaked of their palace on Tumblr from an anonymous account. Below the photo were the typed words: *Ha'alulu Maika'i* (*Figure 43*).

She scrolled up, hoping to see more detailed photos, but only one other image was posted above it in the news feed: the two toucans Silas shaped in the Vortex garden (*Figure 44*). Meg knew it was a message from Silas to her that he still loved her—and her heart swelled with joy in relief.

She printed the image of the palace and toucans and put them in her wallet.

She so wanted to send the photo of the building to the top design magazines, which she loved reading, to show enthusiasts of the profession that a real fantasy building could still be built in the modern age. At the same time, she knew how important Silas' secrecy was—the Touchstone had to be protected for the earth to survive.

She had no idea where the land she had come to call home was on Kauai, but she was determined to find it again.

This time she left her things in good order. She called all her friends and family and told them she was going to see her lover, Silas, on the island of Kauai and couldn't leave an address yet, but she gave them a P.O. Box in Hanalei Bay she had leased over the phone and promised to call soon. She swore she wouldn't disappear into complete obscurity like she did the last time. She explained that she did lie to them at first, but it was only to protect this amazing project Silas and she had been working on at his property.

Putting everything on auto-pay, she left her condo neat and tidy and gave Sam a key to check on things. And, she thought, there might be a way to return to East Hampton one day, now that the building was built. She made Dawn an executor on all her personal accounts and left her with a key to the condo as well. At the office, she appointed Bob, the senior architect in Chelsea, to take charge of the firm until she returned.

A few days later, she was sitting with her feet up and her cow-printed Toms shoes off in a first-class seat on her way to Hawaii, sipping a Perrier with lemon. She had just taken her small Ghurka leather tote bag stuffed with nothing but the whitest clothes she had and her toothbrush.

After a puddle-jumper flight to Kauai from Oahu, she taxied to the Cliffside Resort Hotel. With no way to find Earl, Meg decided she could find the property from the water due to the unique layout of the cove. So, she booked a boat with the concierge for the next day to take her on a survey trip of the entire Napali coast. Hank, a neat, young guy with gelled black hair, said he would arrange it and quoted her the exorbitant fee, which she accepted with a smile. She asked him to add it to her tab.

After having her bags delivered to her room, Meg decided to relax in the lobby. Studying the room, she admired how it was completely opened-up by way of tall, elegant mahogany sliding shuttered doors. Breezes scented with hibiscus from the garden wafted through the space.

As she took in the whole room, she was pleased to see some of her favorite pieces of furniture from McGuire—one that she had recently used in a modern house on the ocean in San Francisco (the home of McGuire furniture).

As she took in the room with its soft, natural dappled light, she drifted more and more into a daydream. As her eyes moved across the room from the sisal rugs on the stone floors to the bamboo chandeliers and palm leaf wall sconces, Meg was no longer there but with Silas. His eyes...

Figure 43 Ha'alulu Maika'i *on Tumblr*

Figure 44 Silas' Toucan Topiary on Tumblr

58

The next morning, Meg woke in the giant bamboo bed in her room and wondered where she was. She suddenly realized she was at the hotel in Kauai. It was Thursday and the first day of April, which meant it was also April's Fools Day. She quietly prayed this was not a joke and that she really was in Kauai on her way to find the Vortex.

Meg jumped out of bed, quickly dressed and taxied to the marina. It was a bright Hawaiian day on the water. Meg and the skipper, a sumo-sized Japanese shirtless guy named Kobe, shook hands in front of his boat. He was wearing rainbow-mirrored deep-sea fishing glasses with black matte wraparound frames. Meg had a one-piece white swimsuit with matching Celine sunglasses, a straw hat and a white surah wrapped around her waist. She had her Ghurka bag in the other hand, just in case they found the cove.

"I'm Meg."

"I'm Kobe."

"Nice, like the beef?"

"Yep, that's me."

"Sweet, I love me some Kobe steak. Do they really make those cows drink beer?"

"Yeah, to fatten them up! And they give them massages. I wish someone would massage me and feed me beer all day. Hahaha. Come aboard Meg!" He hopped into the boat and offered Meg a hand. Taking it, she climbed in. "Hank at the hotel said you want to take a survey trip around the island today?"

"Yeah, that's the idea."

"Okay, sounds good, but you're gonna need some sunscreen."

"I got some just in case."

The pair cruised around the rugged Kauaian coast on very choppy waters for about half an hour with no sign of the cove at all. The waves made Meg so seasick that she ordered Kobe to turn around and head back to the marina for the day. She was still jetlagged from the flight and just needed to rest.

Back in her hotel room, she was on the verge of tears. Although Kobe agreed to try again tomorrow, she didn't know how they could find it. But that cove was so special. She hadn't seen it from the water, only the sand, but the large rock outcropping was like a birthmark on the place, no one could miss it. She decided they would probably find it the next day.

That night, she ordered lomi lomi salmon from room service and a Tai Chi cocktail of spiced rum and pineapple. But, when the food came, she started to cry over the dish that she ate at the Vortex and she couldn't stop the tears once they started. There was a pain deep in her heart for Silas and it hurt when she breathed. She had never missed anyone so much.

She decided to not eat, turned the light off and lay there looking at the ceiling. Finally, she fell asleep into a dream where she saw Silas dressed in white on a beach, walking backwards holding her two hands, grinning joyously. And she felt they would never be apart again. In the distance, the Oli Aloha chant used in Hawaiian weddings was being recited and she knew they were getting married. When she awoke in the morning, she felt exhilarated.

She searched Google for the meaning of the Oli Aloha and found it on a wedding website:

"There was a seeking of a loved one, now she is found. You two are now to become one."

So beautiful, she thought, and closed her laptop.

That day, she and Kobe headed southwest again on calmer water, but went further. After forty-five minutes, the views along this stretch were absolutely stunning. Huge green mountains jutted out to their left, staggering down to the water where they met the ocean. Meg was feeling at home again. The terrain began to look familiar—the scent of the plumeria flower she liked to place behind her ear drifted across her nose. And in a hundred feet, Meg finally spotted the little romantic beach cove from the boat.

"Over there! Over there!" She pointed gleefully. Kobe gladly anchored close to the shore.

"Wait one second, Kobe."

Meg jumped into the water, holding her Ghurka bag high above her head, and rushed for the sand.

Walking up to the gate, she pushed the handle down, but it was locked. Her heart sank. She shook the gate by the bars the same way Red had done, yelling out for help. She was about to turn, when in the distance down the hall, she saw something approaching. She thought it might be a mouse, but as it came into the light, it was one of her iguanas, Tom. She had thought they all looked the same at first, but now she could see the differences, the subtle nuances of the musculatures of their faces and skin shades. Tom raced up to her, said "Howdy lady," and climbed up to the door handle where he knocked the fire poker out onto the ground (Silas had used it as a door lock since Bernie had cauterized it).

"Thank you, thank you, my little green friend."

She opened the door and breathed a sigh of relief. Then she leaned down and let Tom climb up on her arm where she petted him for a while. Then, she set him down and asked, "And just how did you get down here? I mean, I only saw the elevator."

"There is a hole that only I know about, my lady, that goes down the elevator shaft and exits under the mini kitchen sink. You see, there are holes all over the world that only us little guys know about."

Meg laughed. "You're a resourceful little fellow, aren't you?"

"Yeah, I must say I kind of am," he said and winked.

"Well do me favor, and go tell everyone I am here."

"Sure thing my lady. I will be on it lickety split." And he darted back down the hall.

"That's the spirit."

She walked back out onto the warm sand and told Kobe to leave her there—that she would call the hotel to settle up. "I know the owner of the land here. He's my secret boyfriend."

Quite confused, but happy nonetheless, Kobe smiled and yelled out, "All beaches are public in Hawaii anyway, Meg. I can't make you get back in the boat if you don't want to."

"I wouldn't even if you tried."

"Hahaha. Sounds good, girl. Mahalo! Have fun!"

He sped off, leaving her there. She entered the long cave corridor to the circular room and then up the elevator, her heart skipping beats with excitement and joy after every new step. At the top of the elevator, lo and behold, Silas was waiting there to greet her.

"Welcome home, Meg-a-poo."

She fell into his arms crying.

"Am I really home? Is this really me?" she said through the tears. He wiped the moisture from her eyes.

"Yes, you are you and you are here."

She smiled and looked past him to see the entrance of the Theater straight ahead, flanked by rows of date palms.

"Let me give you a tour of the place, sweetheart (*Figure 45*), now that it's finished and landscaped. You'll love the fountains and runnels now that those are up and running as well."

"Oh Silas, I've missed you so much, and I've missed everyone and everything here at the Vortex. I just couldn't even breathe back home. Yes, please show me our wondrous place." And she stared up, her face filling with awe and wonder.

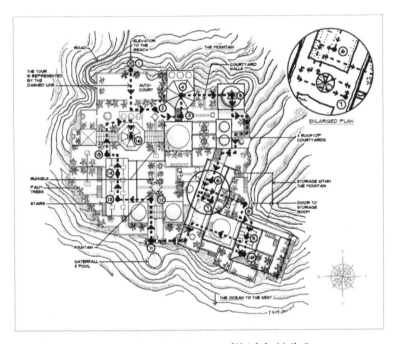

Figure 45 Silas gives Meg a tour of Ha'alulu Maika'i

59

The two walked toward the entrance of *Ha'alulu Maika'i* (*Figure 46*) and Meg glanced to her left, where the Library had giant date palms in its foreground. A quick peek forty-five degrees to the right, and she saw the Office behind a wall surrounded by palm trees.

"Where do we start?" she asked Silas.

"Let's head over to the Library and then take a clockwise tour of all the buildings and courtyards. We'll save the Theater for last—I have a surprise waiting there for you."

"Ok babe. But how did you know I was coming?"

"Why, that little green fellow told me. You know the one, Tom."

"Hahaha." She laughed.

Hand in hand, they walked toward the Theater and turned left. Immediately, Meg was at her favorite spot (number 2 on the tour) where she could see through the palace by way of arched openings all the way down to the ocean below. Except now the sound of running water coming from runnels and fountains, and palm tree alleys and paved courtyards all created a completely magical vision.

"Oh my God Silas—I couldn't have imagined the full effect of this. It's overwhelming to say the least, and it was my baby!"

"It's the *mana* from the Touchstone—that's why I called it *Ha'alulu Maika'i*—and you know what? It's even better looking coming back the other way when we get to the lower level."

Meg glanced over to the Sacred Studies Building (*Figure 47* – number 3 on the tour) from the entrance to the Library and oh, how beautiful it was looking today.

"Let's go into the Library. I know you've seen the 'shell' already, but the shelving and furnishings are truly wonderful."

"Yes, I must see it."

When she entered the main level (number 4 on the tour), the effect of all of the exquisitely made shelves filled with gorgeous old books and manuscripts bound in leather astounded her. They were lit by the softest sunlight coming through the small vertical windows she had designed to limit the effect of harmful ultraviolet rays on the books. The room was magical, not the architecture alone, but the masterful cabinetry, thousands of books, the beautiful plaster walls and the timber ceiling, all touched by the most sensitive rays of sunlight from each wall of the hexagonal room. The grand cast bronze chandeliers that she had designed with various bird silhouettes along the different tiers added to the magical realism of the space.

"We'll see the other floors later. Let's go to the Sacred Arts Building next."

"I can't wait, there's so much to see and take in and we've only just begun."

They walked through a side door to an intimate courtyard with palm trees. Meg always loved seeing the mountain where it was allowed to enter the space on the east wall. But now through the magic of Silas's green thumb, it was covered with lush wildflowers and ferns as well as a perfect specimen maple tree planted in just the right spot. The Sacred Studies Building was straight ahead, and it looked so lovely to Meg, she could actually sense its *baraka*. Something was happening to her that she didn't understand. The fragrances, sounds of the water, palm trees swaying in the warm breezes, the closeness of the beautifully laid stone walls, the roofscapes beyond of domes and barrel vaults, the afternoon sun kissing everything in sight with the most lovely and clear light, and Silas' gentle vibe caused a unique sensation within her. Meg was suddenly overtaken by a sense of euphoria: a oneness with everything. She was perfectly still and staring wide-eyed straight ahead when suddenly Silas quickly shook her body with his hands and said, "Come out of it—there's a time and a place for that...but not here and now."

Crying, Meg said, "Oh Silas, I'm just so full of love right now, I'm so joyous to be back here with you where I was always meant to be. Back home. Just now, I felt like I was about to leave my body. What was happening to me?"

"It's the *mana* and the coalescing of a million magical moments into one. That's what great architecture feels like. And it's the gentle touch of a friend that brings us all back sometimes," he said and winked at her. "You were so happy and so in touch with the cosmos that you could have left us for good right here and now. But I need you. This place needs you."

"Thank you honey, but I shall always remember this precious moment in our garden where I touched heaven even if only for a moment."

"Let's go into the Sacred Studies Building where you will be calmer. It is the place you designed for us to do our meditations and other Inner Work after all."

"Okay, that sounds great."

When they entered (number 5 on the tour), Meg felt the sacred energy of the space immediately. She walked up about twenty steps into the main space and held Silas' hand while she looked up into the dome. It had been painted with the pattern that she had designed, a pattern that had been growing in her imagination until it was fully realized in her mind. As she drew and developed it, she became aware that it had a subtle spiral design buried in its obvious yet beautiful motifs and patterns. The spiral met, framing the huge round skylight (an oculus) that she designed using thick pieces of hand-blown glass held in place by an old Roman formula for cement. The glass pieces were all different sizes and shapes of stars. The entire effect was transformative, and Meg was suddenly at peace and happy to be back on solid Mother Earth.

"It's so peaceful in here, darling," said Silas. "I visit often now when no one else is around, and I feel so grateful to be alive and to have this wonderful building to help us all in our inner journeys."

Meg studied the rest of the space, impressed by the second-level study rooms that wrapped around the perimeter of the large volume. It was made of timber and windows with hand-blown glass. A continuous walkway allowed circulation and access to the rooms. Meg had not seen this before she left, and was mesmerized by how well this wooden architectural device looked and worked on the white plaster walls supported by her stone columns designed with pineapple capitals (*Figure 48*). The pineapples were her idea. She needed a new classical order for this building that represented Hawaii, so she had decided to invent one. And Silas just adored them.

"Let's skip the apartment building that would have been next and go to the one to its west."

"Good, there's a surprise there waiting for you."

"Oh yay, I love surprises!"

They went down a flight of stone steps and through an arched opening into a courtyard. The mountain was to their left and Silas had planted the lushest beds of wildflowers, ferns and other native plantings, which added beauty and fragrance to their descent. They entered the apartment building on its central axis and walked through a dimly lit hall into the building's central sunlit atrium. This was one of Meg's favorite spots.

Meg always had held a special place in her heart for the spaces where human beings lived and were nurtured. She liked the way the apartments looked into the atrium through their large windows (*Figure 49* – number 6 on the tour). The skylight, which was on the building's roof terrace, was made from thick glass shapes held in place by Roman cement. In this case, the shapes were animals, representing the different craftsmen who built the place. This was indeed a special tribute to them from her.

Silas then told Meg, "We're going up to the roof terrace next. You must see the compound from there since it's been completed."

They went up one of Meg's intricate stairs that turned one way and then another to catch the sources of light. Then at the top, they went through a large arched steel and glass window wall onto the roof terrace (number 7 on the tour), where they walked on top of the animal skylight over to the edge where Meg could see the wonders before her: plantings everywhere— huge bougainvillea vines climbing and hanging off the stone walls all around. The perfect amount of bougainvillea. Silas had planted and trained the greenery with his mind to be in only the most ideal spots. Fountains and runnels abounded. Then they went to the other side of the roof to view the rest of the courtyards and plantings. The mountain's sides, with their wildflowers, added a softness to everything. Meg's solid architecture floated in a sea of living nature: color, fragrance and beauty. Bees, butterflies and birds were abundant. In a perfect world, perfect things exist—well not exactly perfect, but rather perfectly imperfect. This was what she had envisioned all along for her masterpiece. But without Silas' magical green thumb this would have never worked. She knew that he knew how it all would turn out. She had felt skeptical but his certainty had been contagious, guiding her through the process.

"Now, my sweet, we'll go straight to our house and visit the next apartment building another day."

"What do you mean *our* house?"

"I mean, it's ours! Yours and mine. Don't be so shy, girl." He kissed her.

"Oh, Silas! Thank you so much." And she hugged him so hard she almost knocked him over.

Just as they were about to enter their house, Meg looked to her left and noticed an old rustic door into the mountain (*Figure 50* – number 8 on the tour).

"What's that?"

"Oh, that's just a door into a storage room where we will be keeping some gold for easy access."

After crossing the threshold, Meg instinctively looked back toward the area they entered into and saw the colorful hand-painted wall tiles that she had designed, as well as the magical arched plaster wall embedded with tiny glass shapes that allowed small shafts of light to enter the space (*Figure 51* – number 9 on the tour).

"Silas, it's so lovely!"

Figure 46 *Meg's masterpiece,* Ha'alulu Maika'i

Figure 47 *View of the Sacred Studies Building from the Library's covered colonnade. Location 3 on tour.*

Figure 48 *Meg's new column order: The order of the pineapple.*

NOTE: ABOVE THIS SPACE IS A FLAT SKYLIGHT
(AT THE ROOF TERRACE) THAT HAS GLASS
ANIMAL SHAPES IN A ROMAN CEMENT CIRCULAR
SKYLIGHT.

THE
APARTMENTS
SURROUND
THIS CENTRAL
ATRIUM

PLASTER
WALLS WITH
STONE TRIM

DOOR
FROM THE
ENTRANCE
HALL THAT
SILAS &
MEG ENTER
FROM

Figure 49 *The central atrium in apartment building #3. Location 6 on tour.*

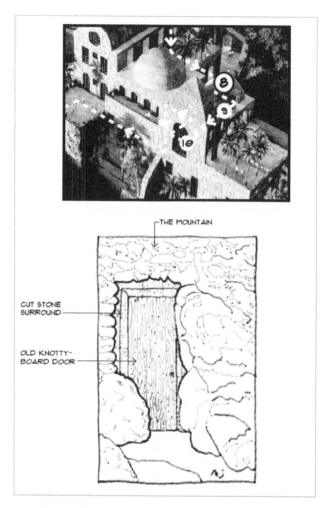

Figure 50 *A door in the mountain into the gold storage room. Location 8 on tour.*

When Meg entered mid-level into the huge foyer that she had designed, she was transported to another time and place, even though she had seen the house many times during its construction. Everything was exotic, old, worn, carved, ornate, gold, silver, and bronze like an antique shop in Marrakech. Rugs, lanterns, African carvings, old paintings of desert tribes; her head spun in amazement.

"Have no fear my darling, come this way." And Silas led her by the hand into the large salon (number 10 on the tour) that looked out over the ocean. The space was as she had designed it, but now had a hand-painted mural around the entire room that depicted exotic locales rendered in an old-world classical technique in sepia tones. Every variety of animal and bird were located among the palm trees, as well as rainforest vegetation. Meg saw all of their construction friends among the wildlife depicted: the iguanas, monkeys, ants, toucans, owls, orang-utans, groundhogs, field mice, squirrels, and more. There was also a hint of her building peeking out from the foliage on one wall and there was an iguana on another, which had to be

Raphael, although he was missing his cigarette. Carlos was swinging from a vine and two toucans were kissing over the main door to the foyer.

Tears of joy fell from her eyes. "Silas, just *who* painted this? It's extraordinary."

"Why our very own Picasso, the toucan Kadiff, painted it all. Even though he's a bird, he's a bit of a savant when it comes to painting. He doesn't have a lick of common sense, and even forgot all of his paints and brushes on the first day! But once he and the crew got started it was a wonder to behold, as you can imagine."

"It's astounding. Now I know why you helped me leave when I did. So you could finish all of this in a magical way and surprise me with the best homecoming any girl could ever hope for. I just love you so much!"

"And I love you and always will." He paused, reaching into his pocket. "I have a gift for you now." He pulled out a ring box and opened it to reveal the most beautiful oval-cut ten-carat diamond ring to Meg. It sparkled in the light of the space. She started bawling her eyes out when she saw it.

"Will you marry me, my love?"

"Yes, yes, I do, I mean, I will!" Meg gushed, throwing her arms around him.

After a moment of holding each other, Silas spoke, "There's so much to see, but we have an engagement in the Theater building, so let's go right over to the observation lookout and have a view up to the compound and mountain to the east. It is a breathtaking sight. Then we'll walk up through the last apartment building and on to the Theater."

Meg agreed and they headed out. They went down to the basement and then used the tunnels from one building to the next to get to the observation point, where Meg again felt overwhelmed. The whole experience was very different than seeing a finished project back in New York. Here, everything felt real, infused by the energy of the stone and the *mana* of the place.

When they finally reached their destination, she pulled herself together and looked around—Silas had planted some type of island cypress trees on the downward slope to the ocean, explaining to her that they helped hide the palace from the outside world. The use of only stone for all of the buildings' surfaces had also helped camouflage the buildings into the mountain, and now all of Silas' plantings had added even more cover.

Meg looked up the center of the main plaza (number 11 on the tour), where she now saw the main runnel and its alley of palm trees, which formed the central axis of the whole layout. It was just as she had envisioned it, and it did precisely what it was supposed to do: bring a unifying clarity to the organizational structure of all the parts. The whole was a gestalt now greater than its parts. And as she looked upward towards the healing mountains and beyond, and saw all of the shapes, forms, and materials forming one harmonious whole, she was happy. A deep sense of peace settled over her and she knew this was home and that she would never leave. She decided to relax and marinate in it all as they walked through the plaza (number 12 on the tour), and Meg saw the exotic sights, heard the birds chirping, the water moving and smelled the flowers' essences.

"Sweetheart, let's go over to the first floor of this apartment building so you can see how truly wonderful it turned out to be. Our community members will enjoy this large space just off the grand plaza for our gatherings and movies—you know how we all love our movies."

They entered the space (*Figure 52* – number 13 on the tour), and Meg was overwhelmed once again by the sheer beauty of the finished materials that she had not seen before she left— the colorful wall tiles and mosaic floors which she had patterned after some Roman tile she had seen in Pompeii on a recent trip to Italy. The framed views out toward the plaza were perfect, as she now so readily expected it all to be.

"Let's go up one level to the main entrance of this building. You'll love seeing how it turned out."

Meg agreed and they used the main stair to the next floor. Upon entering the foyer hall (*Figure 53* – number 14 on the tour), she gasped, "Oh my God, it's so lovely with the southern sun hitting the plaster walls at this time of day. The shadows and subtle light are ethereal. I'm so full of emotion that it will be best if I come back alone to give myself time to absorb and digest every little nook and cranny."

"I am so glad you love it. Now let's go on to the Theater."

They left the building on the east side, and when Meg looked to her left (number 15 on the tour) down to the ocean, she saw what appeared to be the Hanging Gardens of Babylon. Her terraced levels and zigzag perimeter wall design was now covered in exotic flowers and palm trees.

"What a crazy genius you are baby. Thank you for all of this! I couldn't have imagined it in a million years. Let's now go over to the lovely Theater Portico that you designed."

"Okay love. Sounds great," replied Meg.

When they arrived there, while Meg took in the details, Silas said, "Meg, sweetheart, I now have a wonderful surprise for you."

"Oh good, you know how I love surprises."

Silas laughed. "I know, don't we all? It's the magic of knowing that we are on the verge of something amazing but not knowing what that thrills us. Follow me now, love."

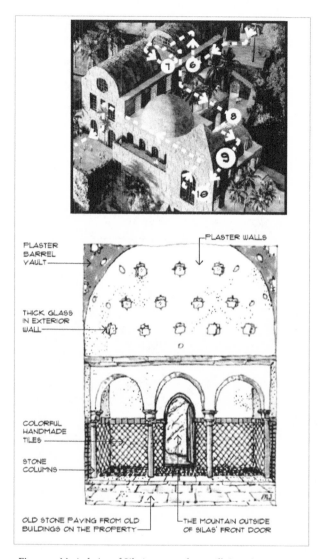

Figure 51 *Meg's design of Silas' entrance door wall. Location 9 on tour.*

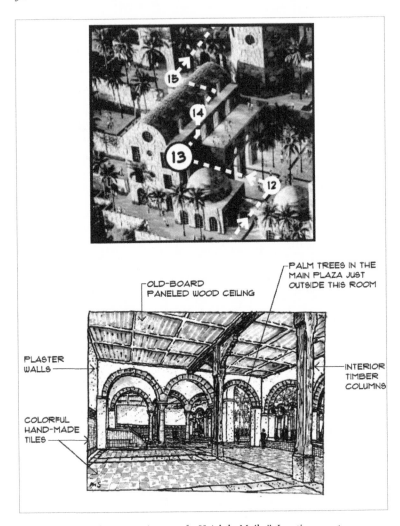

Figure 52 The community room for Ha'alulu Maika'i. *Location 13 on tour.*

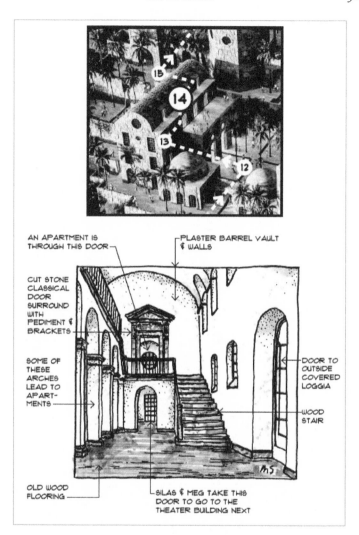

Figure 53 *Entrance Hall in the apartment building #2. Location 14 on tour.*

61

Silas opened the giant carved door of the Theater and Meg stepped in (number 16 on the tour).

A stone masterpiece with its own presence and vibration, Meg wasn't sure exactly how this magical space had come to be, even though she was its *creator*. It almost felt to her like the building had always been there and that she had simply dreamed it. It had its own authentic personality and reality...it was like a parent who comforted and protected you. Its eight tall stone perimeter walls had giant round windows (oculi) high up on each. The sunlight streamed in on long shafts, sharing its illuminating qualities with the hundreds of candles up high in the vast airspace. Lower arched windows brought in filtered light to the seating, which was arranged in eight pie-shapes around the stage.

To her astonished eyes, the entire community of the Vortex, including all the animals and people—Mickey, Eight Foot, Bane, Lono, Kini, Carlos, Banjo, Raphael, Chef Bojangles, Johnnie-O, Kadiff, Chloe, Violet, Kahuna, and all the others—said in unison, "Happy homecoming dear Meg! We love you!"

As tears welled up in her eyes, she replied, "I love you all so much too and I'm so very happy to be back home again. This is where I will always stay, my friends."

Everyone clapped and Silas addressed the assembly. "Meg and I will also be getting married, isn't that right, my dear?"

"Yes," she said, holding up her ring.

The assembly roared with joy and then Silas said, "Hit it, Kahuna."

Frank Sinatra's "Fly Me to the Moon" came on and Silas took Meg's hand. The crowd swooned and the two lovers smiled while they danced on stage with all the lights turned off. And Meg's fantasy was complete, only this time she knew who the man's face was in her dreams. It was Silas.

Shafts of light from the sun, made their way through the round windows, gently lighting the space along with the magical glass stars above. Candelabras from her dreams lit up the dome with its jewel-like structure.

And Meg knew she wasn't just home, she was in love—and not just any love, a love to last a hundred lifetimes.

62

At the end of April, Meg and Silas sat on their favorite rock ledge formation looking out over the ocean. Down below them was Meg's masterpiece, *Ha'alulu Maika'i*.

"I never thought I would ever see this piece of my inner being, my inner architect, come to fruition. If I did, it never matched the actual beauty it now has. You know Silas, we architects are always visualizing perfection, but hoping for only eighty-five percent of our creation to materialize as we *see* it. In this case, the actual building goes beyond my vision. How is that even possible?"

"Well Meg, you put so much of your higher self into your dream of this magical place, that everyone involved in its construction, its materialization, shared that dream with you, and that energy and passion carried us all through its construction with much joy and love for its realization," Silas explained. "For me, and many others here, the time has passed almost magically, as if the building has always been here. Perhaps it *was* always here, and you simply had to see and channel it. This is a gift that you have, and I knew it when I first saw you in my dreams many, many years ago. You have been carrying this edifice within you forever, and now it's here on this plane of reality for us all to enjoy, and for our children to come." Silas paused. "Meg, I must tell you something now that may shock you, but I think the time is right—I am not an old gentleman, I am really 120 years old." Meg gasped and put her hand over her mouth. "My father came here much earlier than I told you. I lied to conceal my real age. I just didn't think you would ever believe me, sweetie.

"If you desire, you shall live here in joy, peace and fulfillment for the rest of your years to protect and guard the Touchstone. The world is a balance of good and bad...but the stone tips the balance by emanating positive energy out into the atmosphere.

"Long after I am dust and bones, you shall teach the ones that come after me how to use it, as I will now teach you. We are all here to create a happier world for humanity with the stone's wondrous healing energy. I think now is the time to tell you that, slowly, you can start to introduce your family and closest friends to the island my love."

Meg cried as she looked out over the ocean. Then she turned and hugged him "Thank you, baby. Thank you for everything. For making all our dreams come true."

APPENDIX I
MAP

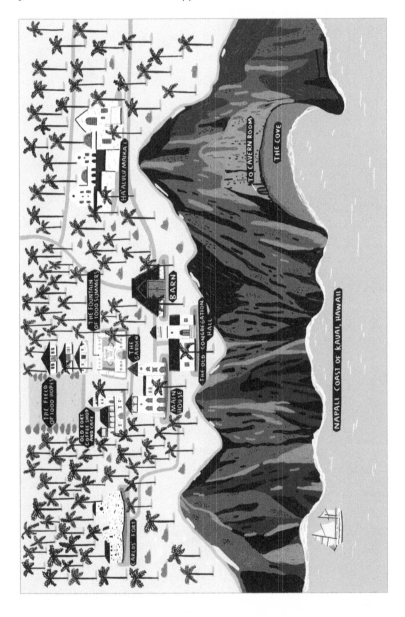

APPENDIX II

Ace – Nineteen-year-old surfer that gets punched in the face by Red.

Ahe – Fernando's right-hand man.

AutoCAD Ants – The crew of architectural ants at the Vortex. Work out of their office, "the Anthill".

Bane – A fit, attractive Hawaiian with a square jaw in his late twenties. Married to his Hawaiian wife Lono. They harvest the fruits and vegetables that grow on the property at the Vortex.

Banjo – Kitchen help to Chef Bojangles. A lanky twenty-two-year-old with a long, black ponytail and a Mediterranean nose.

Beauregard Theodore Bojangles III – The head chef for the Vortex. A walking, talking, cooking alligator from New Orleans.

Bernie – One of the four thieves.

Biscuit - Hawaiian brown mutt dog who lives at the Vortex. He loves raw meat scraps and bones.

Bob – Senior designer at Meg's architectural firm in Chelsea, New York. Meg places him in charge of all the office affairs when she leaves for Hawaii.

Bug – A high school drop-out who has a bad smoking habit and works for the thieves as a "tail".

Camille – The Queen Ant and head of the AutoCAD ants at the Anthill.

Carlos – The orangutan, master stone mason and bosom buddy of Silas. He lives in an old fort on the mountain at the other end of the Vortex.

Chief Riley – Chief of Police in Lihue, Kauai, Hawaii.

Chloe – Cute twenty-something blonde with amber eyes who lives at the Vortex. Has a crush on Mickey.

Dawn – Meg's younger sister who had an affair with Meg's ex-husband, Mick Drewford, ending their marriage.

Dot – Meg's grandmother from Newport, Rhode Island.

Eight Foot – Seven-foot-tall shirtless, barefoot, tattooed Samoan man with a bald head and drawstring pants who resides at the Vortex. He helps lift and move things.

Eric Arakawa – Owner of the Eric Arakawa Surfboard Company, a legendary shaper on the North Shore of Oahu.

Fernando Serrano – Silas' father. A nineteenth-century Spanish adventurer who laid claim to the Vortex after it was abandoned.

Fuzzyhead – Macaque monkey and master timber framer.

Halie – Orangutan master plasterer.

Jake Smith – Coast Guard Officer.

James – Meg Summer's father. He has a bushy brown mustache, well-groomed hair and makes the meanest bowl of New England clam chowder anyone west of Nantucket has ever tasted.

Jim Flush – Kauaian police officer.

Johnnie O – Groundhog master plumber.

Juan Cordoba – Simon's brother and Spanish crew member who set foot on Kauai in the sixteenth century.

Kadiff – The toucan and master painter who paints like Picasso.

Kahuna – Coffee barista at the Vortex, serving up the good stuff all day long.

Kala – Fernando's Hawaiian wife.

Kini – Native Hawaiian who lives at the Vortex and works the gold mine. He traces his roots back to the first well-known Hawaiian surfer, Duke Kahanmoku.

Kobe – Shirtless Japanese sumo-size skipper who takes Meg to search for the Vortex by boat.

Larry – Bernie's brother who co-owns Island Jewelry in Kauai. Has a pot belly and wears a large gold necklace and reading glasses. Accomplice to Red's crew of misfits.

Mallory (Mal) Jackson – Meg's genius head designer and Yale graduate who only wears black clothing. She is slender, has black spiked hair, no make-up, a constant frown, a fairy-like angelic face, and argues about absolutely everything.

Meathead – A muscle-bound Polish thief with a bald head.

Meg Summers – Thirty-seven-year-old principal architect of Summers & Co. in East Hampton, New York. She got divorced from her husband, Mick Drewford, a year ago after she caught him having an affair with her sister Dawn. A creative soul who tells everyone she is "born to draw", she never misses a day of work, even when she is sick. Sent for by Silas to draw a fantastical building for the Vortex.

Mickey aka Mr. Sun – Blond-haired surfer who lives at the Vortex. Drives a beat-up white Toyota four-door Tacoma and helps Chef Bojangles in the kitchen on most evenings.

Mitch – Meg's regular waiter at the Saltbox Café—a surfer with shaggy brown hair and blue eyes.

Mitch Franks– FBI agent investigating the robbery at Andy's Gold.

Mick Drewford – Meg's ex-husband and one of the snobbiest guys at Yale.

Mr. Bartholmey (Bart) – A mainstay in East Hampton, he owns Meg Summer's favorite rare bookstore, The Nook & Cranny.

Mugshot – Getaway driver for Red's crew.

Nathan – Vortex resident librarian who is always found with a book in his hand. A quiet, introverted guy from Ohio with a big bush of black hair, he would rather read than talk.

Officer Henry – Square-faced macho Hampton cop who investigates Meg's disappearance.

Officer Matt Rogers – The lead detective for the Kauaian Police Department, investigating the robbery case at Andy's Gold store.

Peggy – Meg's charming secretary, who always makes Meg laugh.

Raphael – Iguana head mason who smokes too much.

Ray Nestle – Coast Guard Officer

Red Robinson – Skilled Aussie thief with a tattoo of Poseidon on his right forearm and a long scar on his cheek.

Ronald – Crooked employee at Andy's Gold.

Sam Babson – Meg's most stylish gay renderer from Dothan, Alabama, who still draws by hand, the old-fashioned way.

Samantha – The white owl, master electrician and solar expert.

Scarlett – Meg's mother who lives in Newport, Rhode Island, in a historic house by the ocean.

Silas – aka "Man of the Woods", is the Guardian at the Vortex for the Touchstone. An elegant, aristocratic Spanish gentleman who is lean with a serious eye. Can control the weather, read minds, communicate with and control animals and see into the future due to the powers of the Touchstone.

Simon Cordoba – Spanish stone mason crew member who set foot on Kauai in the sixteenth century. First owner of the Vortex land.

Summers & Co. Architects – Meg Summer's architectural firm in East Hampton, New York.

Tom – White guy with a curly brown crown of hair and horn-rimmed glasses from Buffalo, New York, who manages the grounds at the Vortex. Likes papayas and mangos.

Tua – Short Hawaiian store clerk with a grizzly smile who works at Island Jewelry.

Violet – Chloe's best friend at the Vortex.

APPENDIX III
HAWAIIAN TERMS & SLANG

86 – Slang for "doing away with".

Akai, ekua, ekolu – "One, two, three" in Hawaiian.

Ha' alulu Maika'i – Hawaiian for "Good Vibrations", it is the dream building Meg designs for the community at the Vortex. An illustrious compound of stone buildings with domes and towers that scales up the mountain.

Haole – Hawaiian for anyone who isn't a native Hawaiian, mainly used to denote white people.

Hodad – Hawaiian slang for someone who hangs out at the beach, but doesn't surf.

Imu – Hawaiian underground oven.

"Jake" – Someone who is an inexperienced surfer and interferes with seasoned wave-riders.

Kalua pig – Roasted pig cooked in the ground in an imu and covered with big banana leaves.

Kauai – Hawaiian island in the Central Pacific nicknamed "the Garden Isle" due to the tropical rainforest covering much of its surface.

Lilikoi – Passion fruit.

Lomi Lomi Salmon – A Hawaiian side dish made from salted uncooked salmon, tomatoes, onions and green onions.

Mana – Hawaiian for the spiritual life force that permeates the universe.

Mauka rain – Hawaiian for "mountain rain."

Moas – Hawaiian for "wild chickens."

Moke – A tougher than tough Hawaiian guy.

Oli Aloha – Chant used in Hawaiian weddings: "There was a seeking of a loved one, now she is found. You two are now to become one."

Pakalolo – Hawaiian word for "marijuana."

Plumeria flower – Floral symbol of birth and love. Often tucked behind women's ears in Hawaii.

Poi – A thick paste baked and pounded from the underground stem of the taro plant.

Seashell lei – Lei with black and pink Ni'ahu shells from the Forbidden Island.

Tuna poke – Marinated sashimi tuna. A traditional Hawaiian salad of raw tuna marinated in soy sauce, sesame oil and onions.

APPENDIX IV
POEMS

Four Stones
By Silas Serrano

In the beginning
four exotic stones
buried deep in the earth

at four corners
Hawaii
Iceland
Africa
Peru
to be found
to be touched
to be harnessed
by soothsayers
for the whole world
the colors so beautiful
the sounds so sweet
the power unstoppable

balancing yin and yang
healing the sick
divining time
foretelling
a universe
destined for
Glory

<u>Man of the Woods</u>
By Meg Summers

In a beautiful garden he grows
A flower turned towards the sun
His eyes the color of chocolate cosmos
His lips the shade of a desert rose
His skin the color of honey
And if he cries, Bulgarian rose oil falls down his nose
And there is sandalwood along his neckline
That smells like ancient civilizations
Where the essences of flowers were like gold
And his breath is lavender
Like Maui in the summer where horses still run wild
And he imprints the air with the scent of a thousand flowers
Of every shape and color
And his heart is a garden of roses
That will never wilt with the changing seasons
And in the center lies a perfectly formed one
He waters with his dreams
And the seeds of yesterday that
Never bloomed got blown away with the wind
Into the turquoise sea below
And when the rain falls from heaven he grows
With that spiritual nutrition that only the angels know.

APPENDIX V
FIGURE INDEX

Figure 9 Meg's dream about *Ha'alulu Maika'i* - 3rd sketch —Ken Tate

Figure 10 Theater sketch showing its hexagonal shape and its elegant dome all built out of the same stone.—Ken Tate

Figure 11 A more developed site plan.—Ken Tate

Figure 12 A more developed overall view of *Ha'alulu Maika'i* as it comes to life.—Ken Tate

Figure 13 Phases of construction 1-4—Ken Tate

Figure 14 The fort house for Carlos and his large extended family—Ken Tate

Figure 15 List of artisan categories and their construction schedule

Figure 16 Animal Artisans—Ken Tate

Figure 17 Animal Artisans—Ken Tate

Figure 18 Meg's sketch for the first excavation, and Raphael, the head iguana—Ken Tate

Figure 19 Mountain coming into the Library basement —Ken Tate

Figure 20 Stone #1—Ken Tate

Figure 21 Stone #2—Ken Tate

Figure 22 Stone #3—Ken Tate

Figure 23 Stone #4—Ken Tate

Figure 24 Locations of the four types of stone patterns —Ken Tate

Figure 25 Meg's sketches on 3-D models prepared by the Anthill—Ken Tate

Figure 26 Meg's sketches on 3-D models prepared by the Anthill—Ken Tate

Figure 27 Meg's sketches on 3-D models prepared by the Anthill—Ken Tate

Figure 28 Meg's sketches on 3-D models prepared by the Anthill—Ken Tate

Figure 29 Meg's sketches on 3-D models prepared by the Anthill—Ken Tate

Figure 30 Meg's sketches on 3-D models prepared by the Anthill—Ken Tate

Figure 31 A beautiful drawing by the ant artist extraordinaire, T. Scott Carlisle—T. Scott Carlisle

Figure 32 A front elevation of the entire building compound by the ant artist extraordinaire, T. Scott Carlisle—T. Scott Carlisle

Figure 33 Theater dome design and sketch—Ken Tate

Figure 34 Meg's barrel vault construction sketch for the mason's monkey crew—Ken Tate

Figure 49 The central atrium in apartment building #3. Location 6 on tour.—Ken Tate

Figure 50 A door in the mountain into the gold storage room. Location 8 on tour.—Ken Tate

Figure 51 Meg's design of Silas' entrance door wall. Location 9 on tour.—Ken Tate

Figure 52 The community room for *Ha'alulu Maika'i*. Location 13 on tour.—Ken Tate

Figure 53 Entrance Hall in the apartment building #2. Location 14 on tour.—Ken Tate

Map by Alex Foster

NOTES

Chapter 36

1. See *Figure 24* for the location of the four stone types.

ABOUT THE AUTHOR
KEN TATE

Ken Tate is a well-known architect who finds truth, beauty and soul in architecture. He has been published extensively over his career. Dividing his time between New Orleans and Southeast Florida, he enjoys looking at old houses, cinema, painting, writing and the beach.

facebook.com/kentatearchitect

twitter.com/tatearchitect

instagram.com/kentatearchitect

pinterest.com/kentate

ABOUT THE AUTHOR
DUKE TATE

Duke Tate was born in Mississippi where he grew up surrounded by an age-old tradition of storytelling common to the deep South. He currently lives in Southeast Florida where he enjoys fishing, surfing, cooking Asian food and reading.

You can view his YouTube channel here: http://bit.ly/DukeTateYT and his author website here: https://www.duketateauthor.com/.

amazon.com/Duke-Tate

pinterest.com/duketate786

ALSO BY KEN TATE

New Classicists: Ken Tate Architect, Volume 1

New Classicists: Ken Tate Architect, Volume 2

The Classic House—Windy Hill: Ken Tate Architect

A Classical Journey: The Houses of Ken Tate

The Alchemy of Architecture: Memories and Insights from Ken Tate

The House of Shadows and Light

Coming Soon:

Ken Tate in B & W: Architecture from a Cinematic Perspective

The Architect: Paris Plan

ALSO BY DUKE TATE

With Ken Tate

The Alchemy of Architecture: Memories and Insights from Ken Tate

The Pearlmakers

Book 1: The Hunt for La Gracia

Book 2: The Dollarhide Mystery

Book 3: Gold is in the Air

The Pearlmakers: The Trilogy

Big John Series

Big John and the Fortune Teller

Big John and the Island of Bones

My Big Journey

Returning to Freedom: Breaking the Bonds of Chemical Sensitivities and Lyme Disease

Gifts from A Guide: Life Hacks from A Spiritual Teacher

Quantum Healing: A Life Full of Miracles

Short Reads

Bottom of the Ninth

The Burger Flip Kid

Translations

Gifts from A Guide: Life Hacks from A Spiritual Teacher - Spanish edition

Gifts from A Guide: Life Hacks from A Spiritual Teacher - Dutch edition

Big John and the Fortune Teller - Thai edition

Quantum Living: A Life Full of Miracles - Spanish edition

Coming Soon

Big John and the Hitcher

Big John's Misadventures

The Cobbler

The Wordsmith

The Architect: Paris Plan